A Small Change

Finding the Joy in Everyday Things

Rae-hyeon Kim

TUTTLE Publishing

Tokyo | Rutland, Vermont | Singapore

How To Tie Short Hair

This year's summer

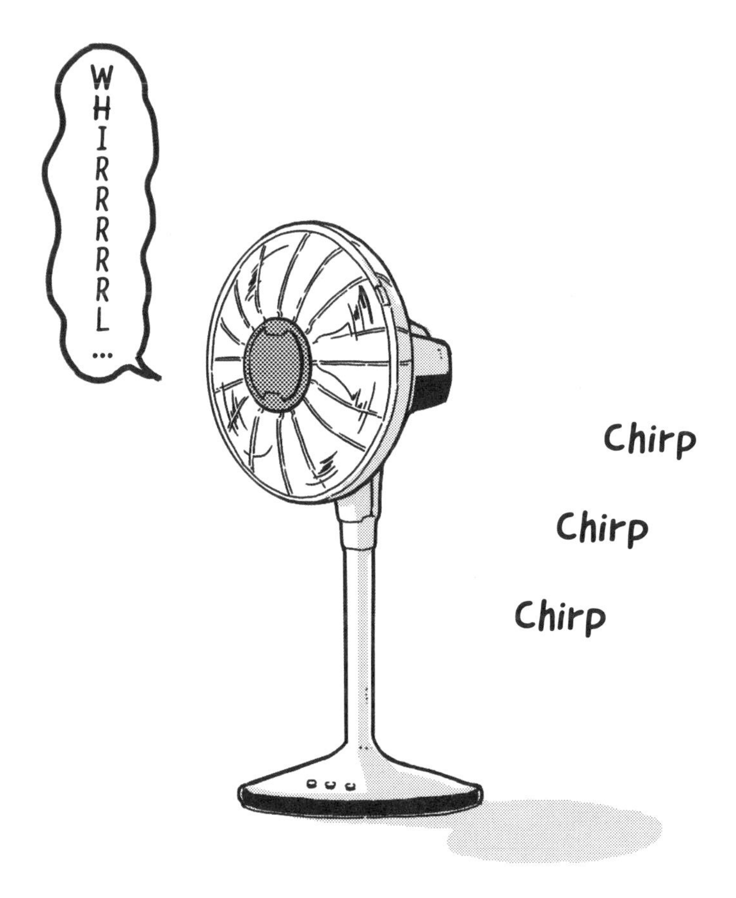

is especially hot.

Chirp
Chirp
Chirp
Chirp
BZZT, BZZT
Extreme Heat Warning Message
2023 July 25th
[Ministry of Public Safety and Security]
Heat Warning, Seoul, Kyeong-gi Province
Please refrain from spending time outside.
고객님께
전기요금 청구서
청구내역
SG TELECOM
Tap, tap
새우
Chana
WHIRRRRRL

Because these days I don't even have time to get a haircut

My hair has gotten pretty long.

Why is this length considered to be pretty long?

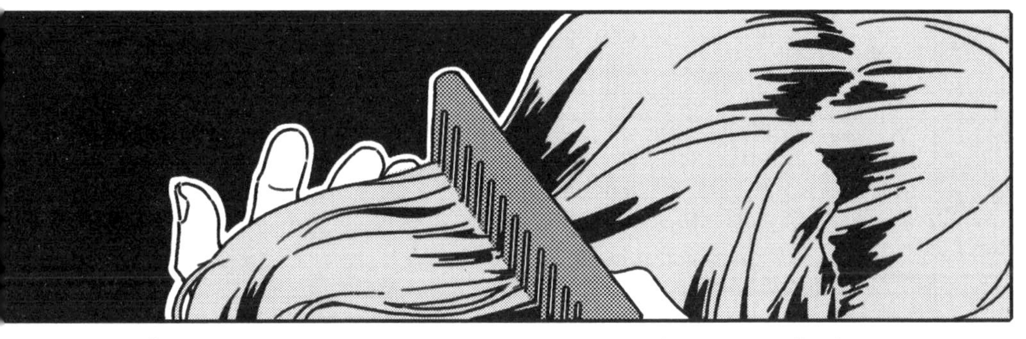

Of course, there was a time when my hair was really long.

My mom would part my hair in waves

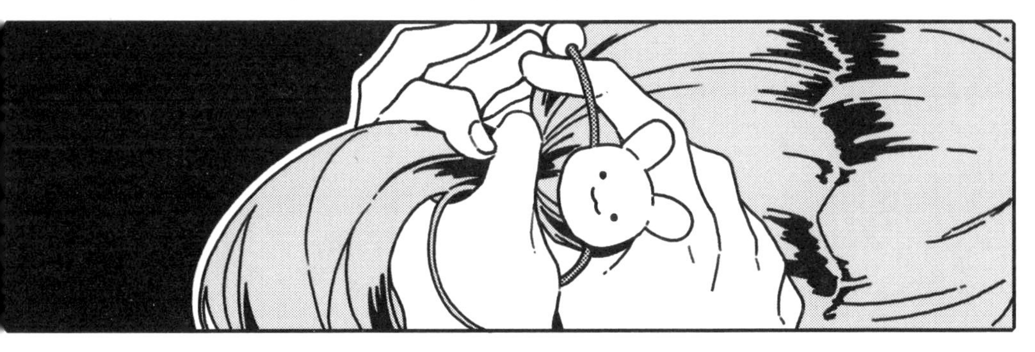

And pull it together so tightly I could feel it in the corner of my eye.

Well, that was only for a little while.

As soon as I was old enough to decide for myself...

...I insisted on keeping my hair short year-round.

Sigh
Anyways, as long as you're alive
the nails on your hand, your toenails, and hair continue to grow.
I SHOULD CUT MY NAILS.
Growl

......
Stands
Click
HMM. BUT TO STAY ALIVE, YOU HAVE TO EAT.
Click
SINCE IT'S KIND OF LATE
Click
I'LL BUY SOMETHING TO EAT FIRST...
Click
23
Scratch
Make a hair salon appointment
Close
Push
Ring

IT'S NICE AND COOL INSIDE.
WELCOME.
WHAT ELSE WAS I GOING TO BUY?
김치
AM I FORGETTING ANYTHING?
Flap-flap

I'M ALMOST OUT OF COKE... WET WIPES...
AND...
1.500
Hair Ties
1.000
Bobby Pins
PONY TAIL
2.500
1+1
......

I bought them.

An impulse purchase can brighten your day.

*around $1

How To Tie Short Hair

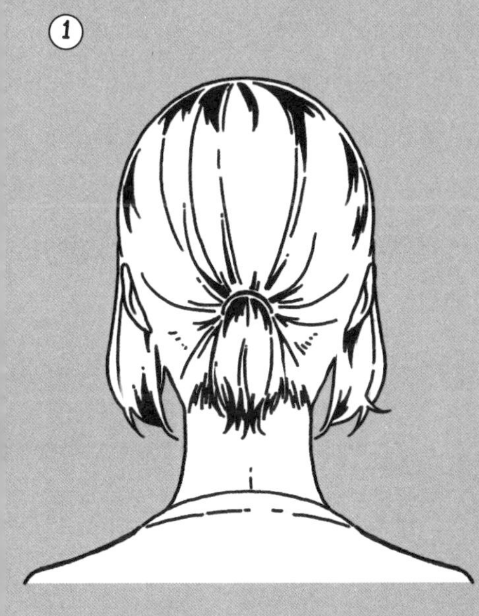

First, brush your hair back. Then leave the front pieces and tie the back pieces together.

2

Then, tie the front pieces together. To create a little volume on the sides, tie it loosely. Tuck in stray pieces.

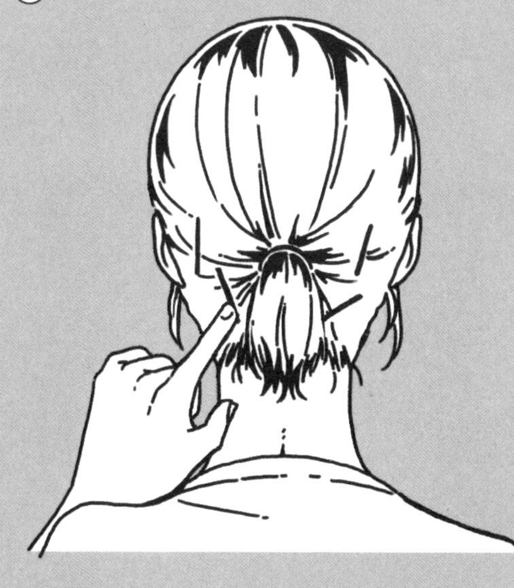

For the stray pieces that escape because they're too short, you can leave them as they are or secure them with bobby pins. It's alright to have some stray pieces. Whatever looks natural.

The breeze I can feel on the back of my neck thanks
to this little hair tie is kind of nice.

Maybe I'll push back the hair appointment.

How To French Braid Short Hair

If things were going according to plan, today would be the day I cut my hair but I canceled the appointment.

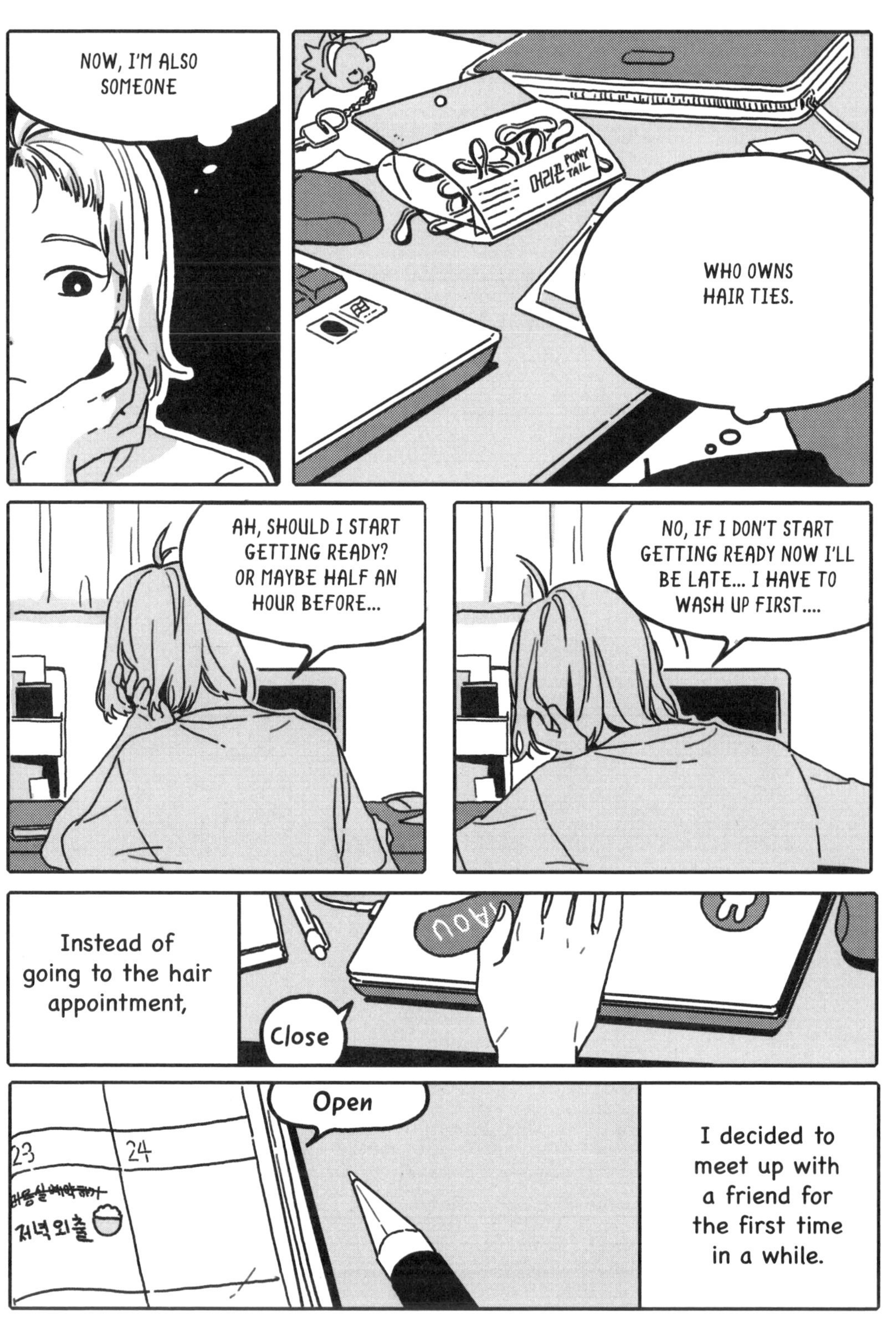
NOW, I'M ALSO SOMEONE
머리끈 PONY TAIL
WHO OWNS HAIR TIES.
AH, SHOULD I START GETTING READY? OR MAYBE HALF AN HOUR BEFORE...
NO, IF I DON'T START GETTING READY NOW I'LL BE LATE... I HAVE TO WASH UP FIRST....
Instead of going to the hair appointment,
Close
Open
23
24
저녁 외출
I decided to meet up with a friend for the first time in a while.

Of course, it's nice to dress casually and leave the house as you are

But once in while I feel the need to dress up. It's self-care.

WHIRRRRRRRRRRRRRRRRL
IT'S HOT....
PRESS
HMM...
CURLS
IT LOOKS WEIRD.

Oh no—I forgot!

It's monsoon season!

In this moment, I realize how powerless humans are in the face of nature.

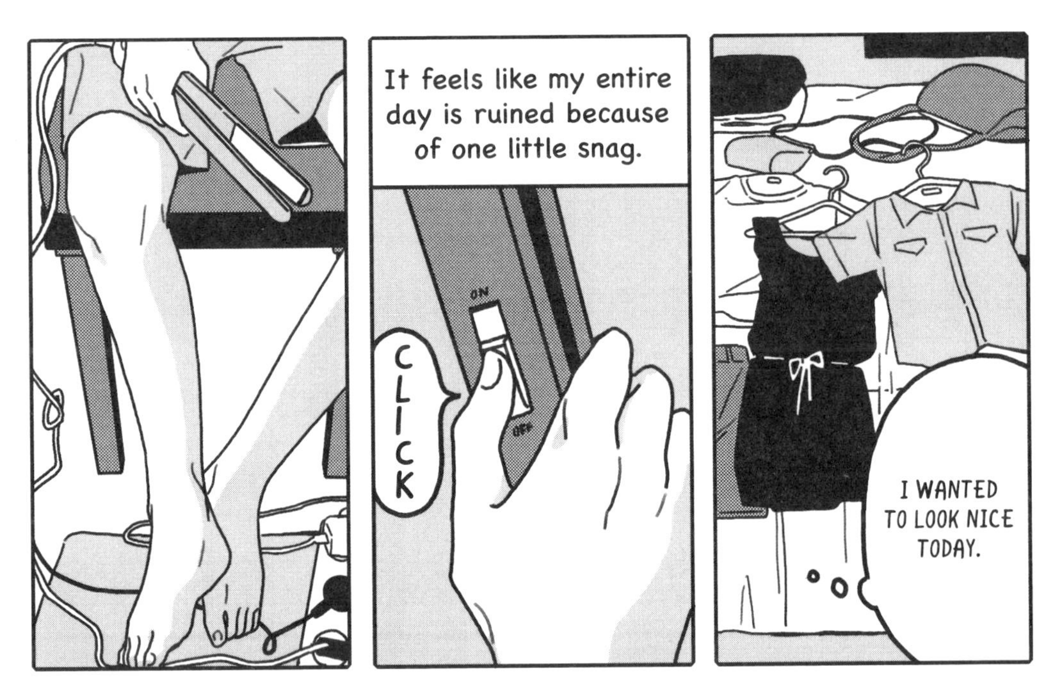

At times like this, you can make a small change.

How To French Braid Short Hair

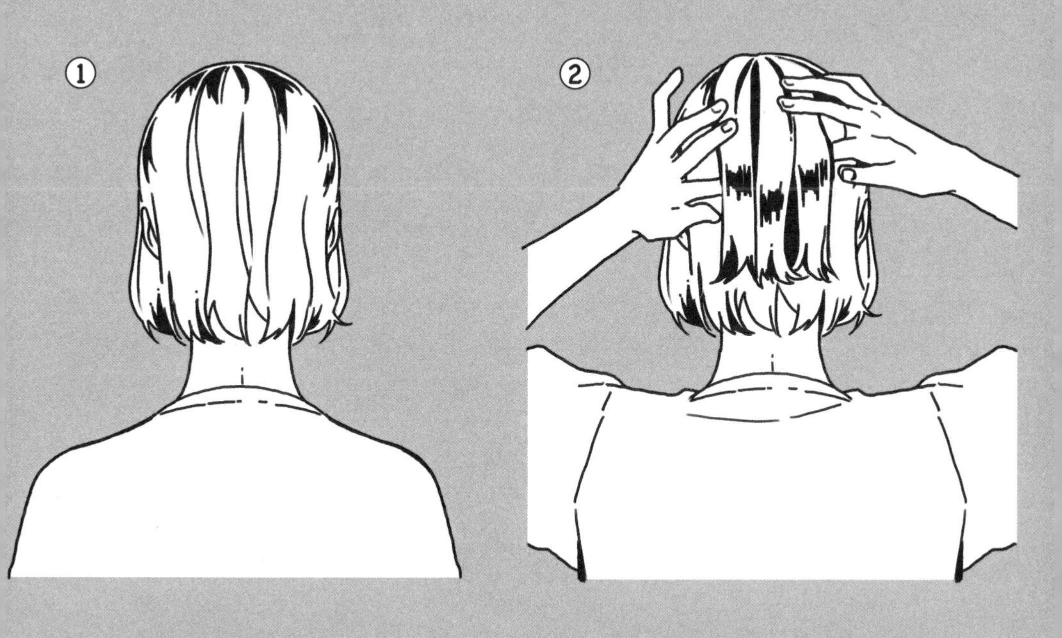

Brush your hair and organize it neatly.

From near the top of your head, take three even portions of hair.

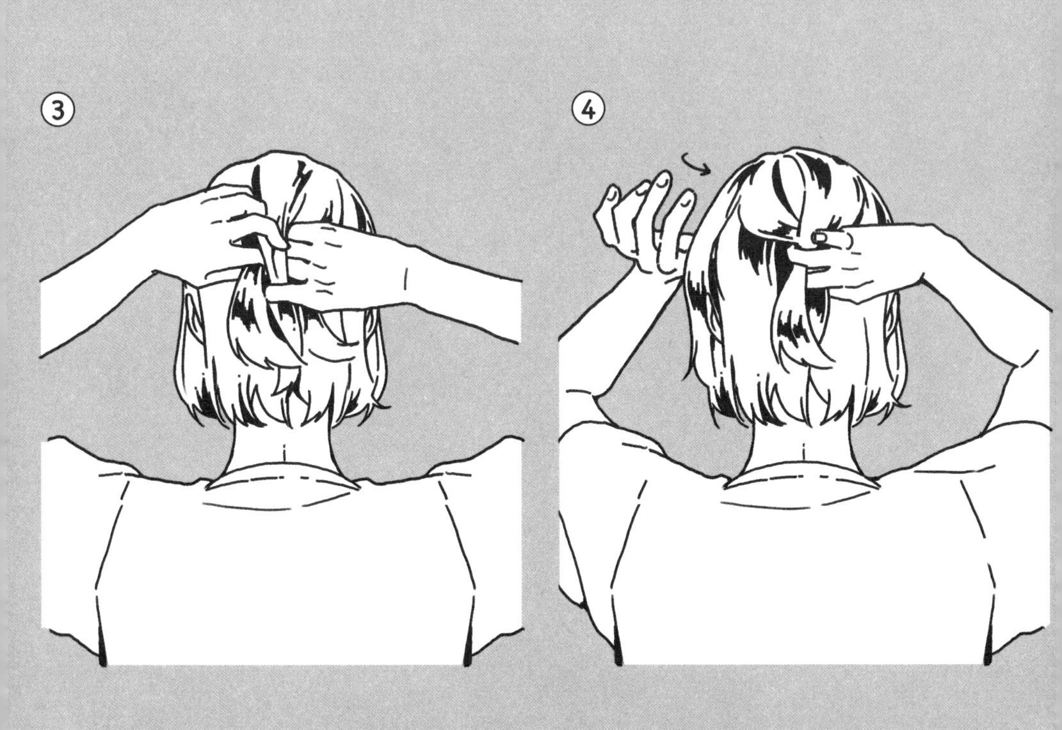

Start braiding them.

Continue moving down while braiding and pull in remaining strands to braid together.

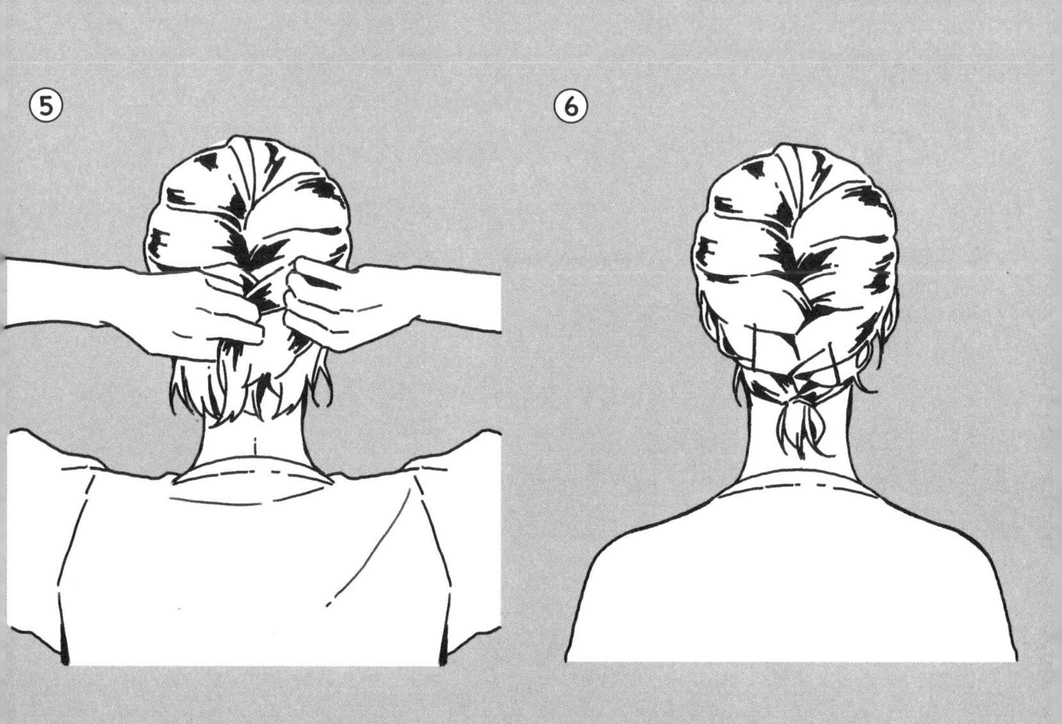

It's important to pull the strands up and braid as if you're stacking them. Repeat until there's no hair left.

After tying together the end with a hair tie, secure the stray hairs with bobby pins.

DID I GO A LITTLE OVERBOARD?
...HMM.
WHO CARES. IT'S MY HAIR, THE WAY I LIKE IT.
OOF.
FROM NOW ON, LET'S CHANGE CLOTHES FIRST AND THEN DO THE HAIR.

fwip
fwip

LOOK WHO IT IS!
I ALMOST DIDN'T RECOGNIZE YOU. YOU TIED YOUR HAIR!
YEAH. I'M TRYING TO GROW IT OUT.
IT SUITS YOU.
SHOULD WE GET SOMETHING TO EAT?

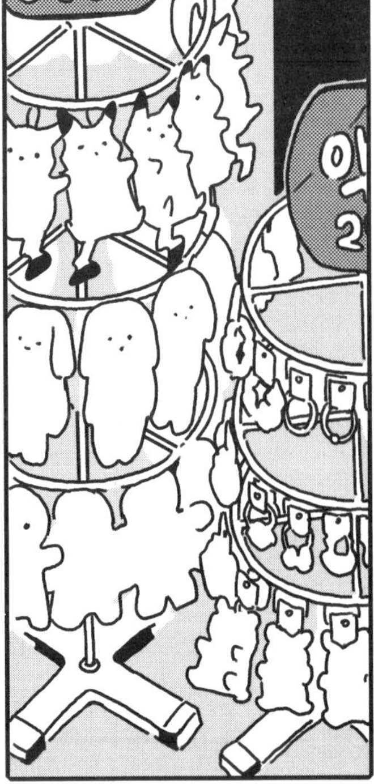
3.000

SLURRP
HAVING MY HAIR TIED KIND OF FEELS LIKE WEARING NEW SHOES.
YEAH?
IT'S THE FEELING WHEN THE HEEL AREA IS STILL STIFF SO YOU NOTICE IT ALL DAY LONG.
AHH.

BUT DOESN'T IT FEEL GOOD TO BE WEARING PRETTY, NEW SHOES?
YEAH.
IF I KEEP WEARING THEM, THEY'LL GET BROKEN IN.
……
....YEAH.
Rainy days aren't so bad.

How To Do A Half-Up Half-Down Hairstyle For Short Hair

Eating is a basic necessity of life, but ironically,
it's is a most difficult task.

RATTLE
IT'S MY DAY OFF...
I KIND OF WANT TO MAKE
SOMETHING TO EAT...
....

Tap
HM...
Tap
머리끈 PON TAIL

How To Do A Half-Up Half-Down Hairstyle For Short Hair

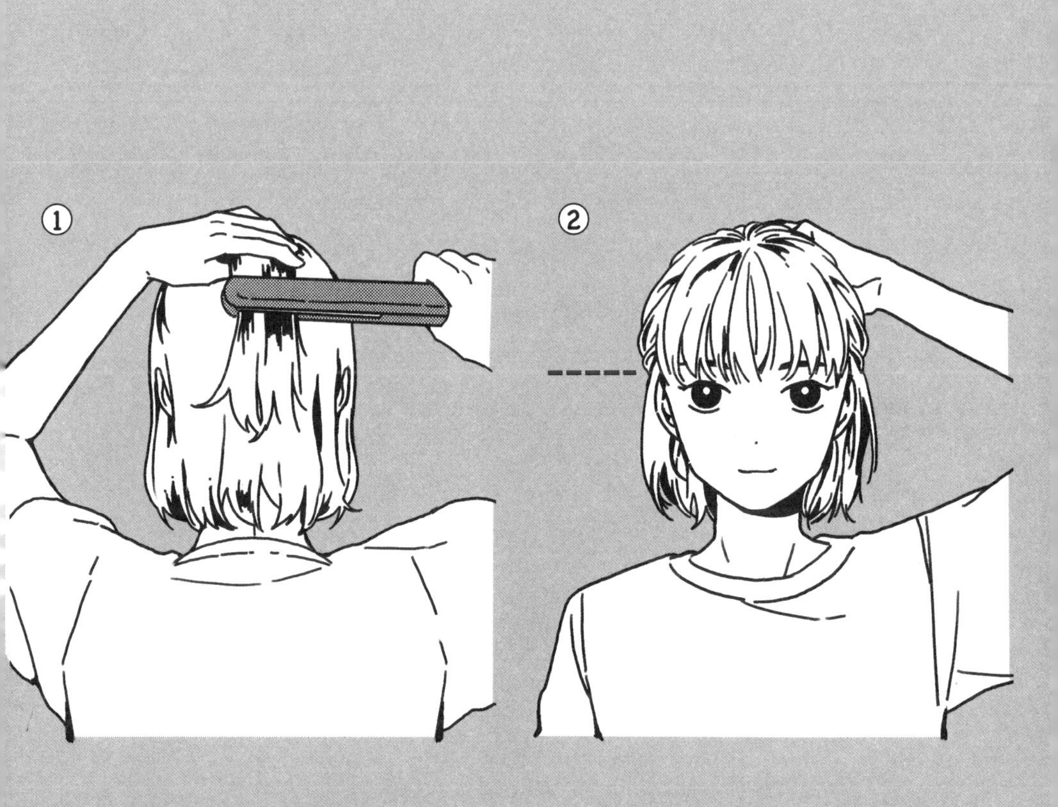

① Add a slight curl to the base of the portion of hair that's going to be tied.

② Position the base of the ponytail higher than the eyebrows, and gather the hair together.

Once you have the position,
tie the hair together.

Straighten your bangs, and
bring out some wisps.

Curl the back pieces and front pieces with a hair iron. After curling with the iron, if you hold the shape with your hand while it cools, the curls will hold.

Twist stray strands of hair and secure with a bobby pin.

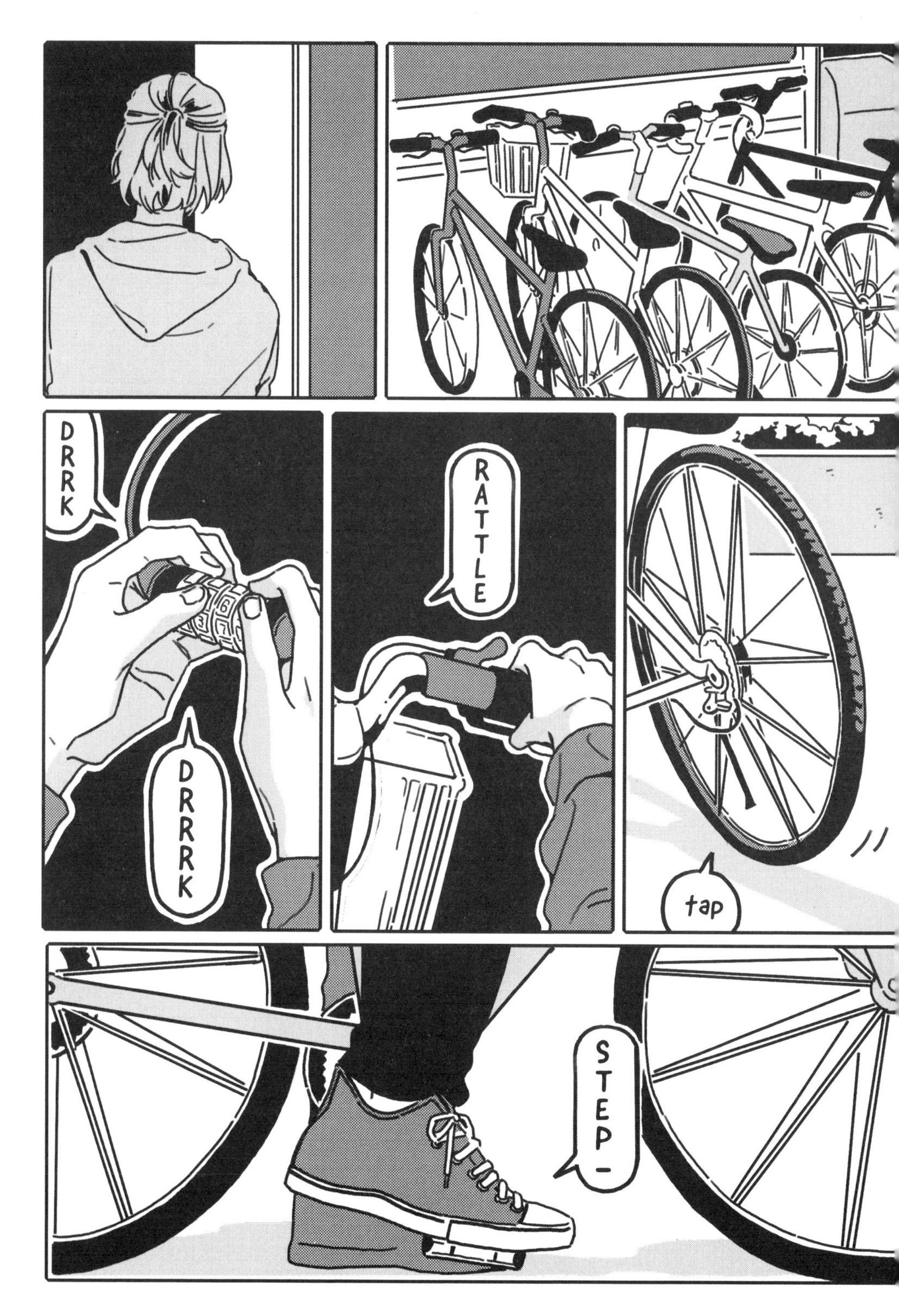
DRRK
DRRRK
RATTLE
tap
STEP-

SUPER MARKET
tap
tap
싱싱
야채
One Serving of Curry
blog

RATTLE
RATTLE
SWIISSSH

toss
rustle, rustle

순후추
카놀라유
blog
SHWAAAAAA
chop, chop, chop ...

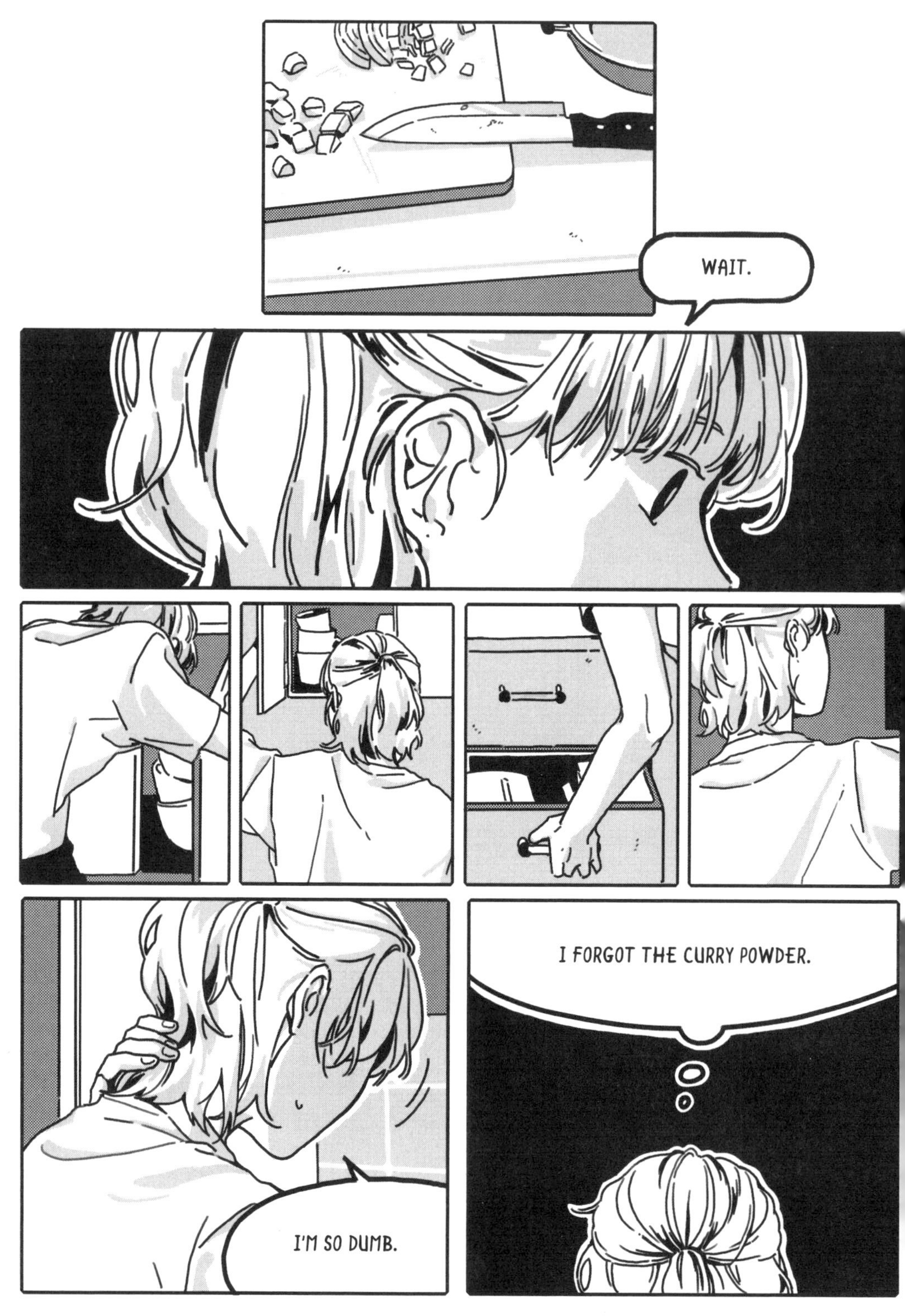
WAIT.
I'M SO DUMB.
I FORGOT THE CURRY POWDER.

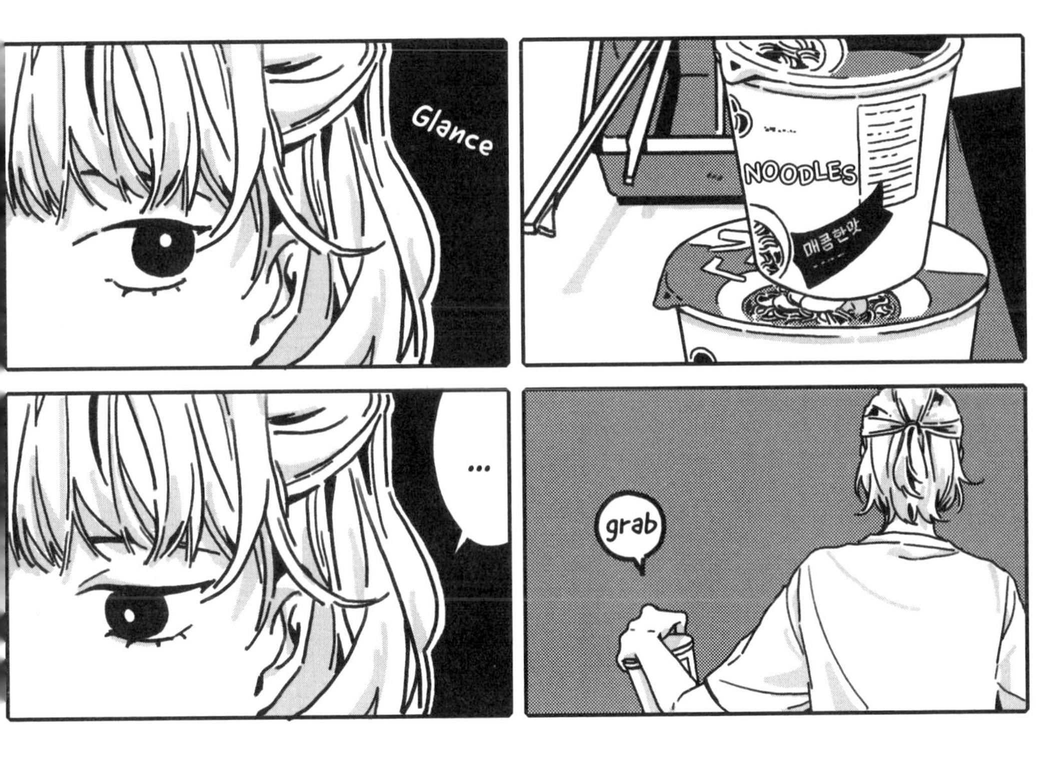

Forcing yourself to do things you don't feel like doing is bad for your mental health

So whatever.

How To Tie Pigtails With A Twist

Okay, perfect.

Now, I just need to do my hair.

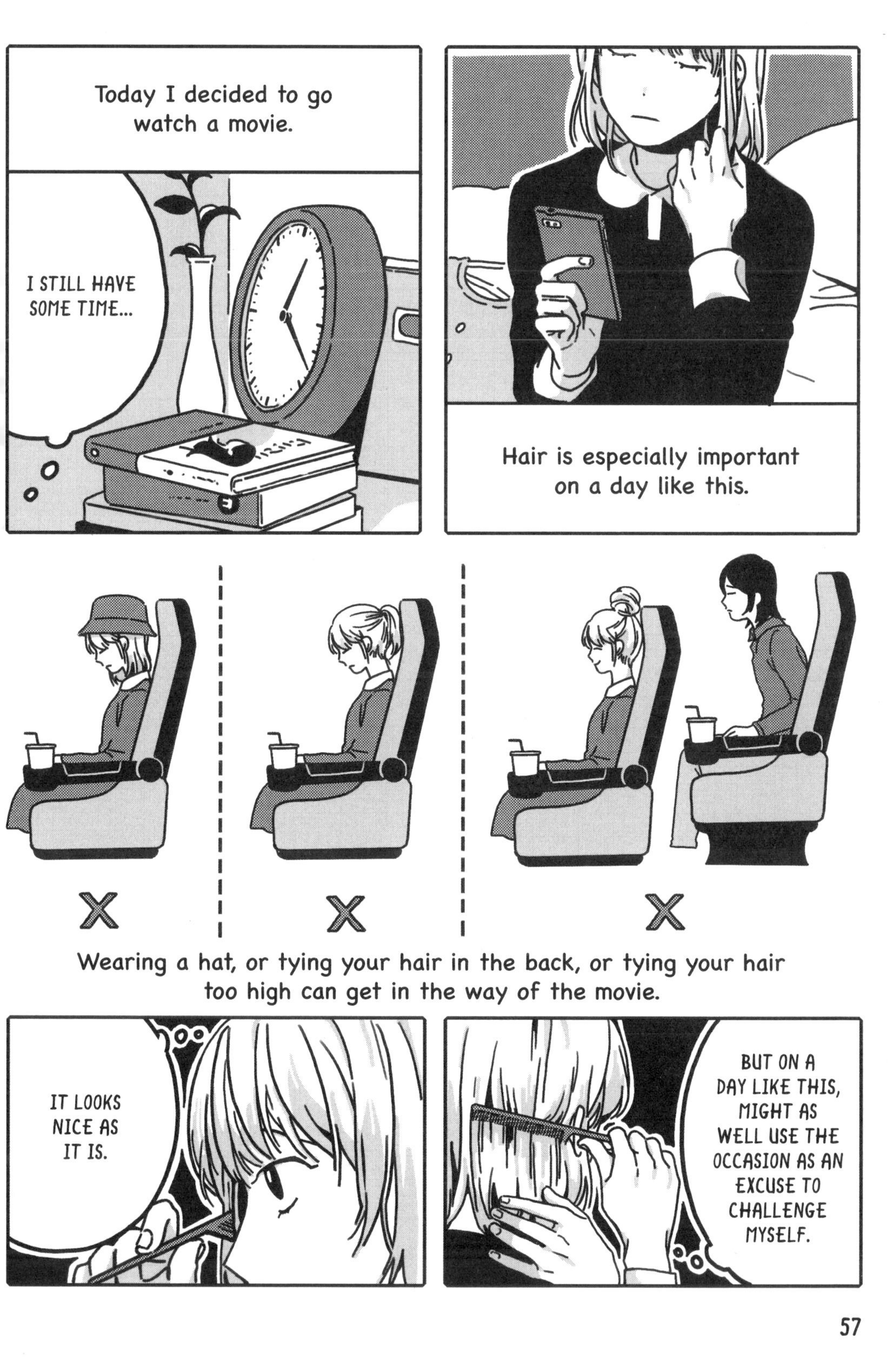
Today I decided to go watch a movie.
I STILL HAVE SOME TIME...
Hair is especially important on a day like this.
Wearing a hat, or tying your hair in the back, or tying your hair too high can get in the way of the movie.
IT LOOKS NICE AS IT IS.
BUT ON A DAY LIKE THIS, MIGHT AS WELL USE THE OCCASION AS AN EXCUSE TO CHALLENGE MYSELF.

How To Tie Pigtails With A Twist

Brush your hair neatly.

②

Lightly grab a front strand of hair and twist it to your ear.

③

Gather small strands and continue to twist the hair.

④

Tuck behind the ear and secure with bobby pins.

After securing both sides,
divide your hair into three
sections and braid together.

⑥

Finish by loosening up any plaits
that were braided too tightly.

BEEP
지하철입구
BEEP
성형외과
EVERYONE GOES BELOW GROUND, THEN BACK ABOVE GROUND — UP, DOWN, UP, DOWN...
I'M ALREADY EXHAUSTED TO DEATH.

TICKET
부인티켓발권기
I'LL GET THE TICKETS. YOU GUYS GET THE SNACKS.
ONE LARGE POPCORN AND ONE DRINK PER PERSON, RIGHT?
I WANT GARLIC BUTTER FLAVOR POPCORN.
CARAMEL POPCORN.
....REGULAR.
....
SHOULD WE GET HOT DOGS INSTEAD?
SURE.

ziiiiing
HUH, WHAT AM I DRINKING?
SPRITE FOR YOU, COKE FOR US.
SPRITE, OF COURSE. IT'S THE BEST!
NOPE. COKE IS THE BEST.
OUR THEATER IS UPSTAIRS, LET'S GO.

Pop!
화장실 ←

WHAT DID YOU THINK OF THE MOVIE? DID YOU LIKE IT?
rumble
SO-SO. BUT IT WAS PRETTY ENTERTAINING.
I THOUGHT IT WAS JUST OKAY.
LIES. YOU WERE CRYING YOUR EYES OUT.
..
OKAY BUT CAN'T THEY MAKE BETTER FEMALE CHARACTERS?
YEAH, RIGHT. THAT WAS A LITTLE...
BUT I LIKED THAT ONE SCENE. WHERE THEY SUDDENLY APPEARED AND
COFFE

OH, SINCE IT'S KIND OF AN AWKWARD TIME SHOULD WE GET COFFEE FIRST?
SURE, I'M DOWN. I'M NOT HUNGRY.
ME TOO.

STAB

YOU SAID YOU WEREN'T HUNGRY.
......

NOW THAT I'M REALLY LOOKING I SEE YOUR HAIR HAS GROWN OUT QUITE A LOT.
OH YEAH.
IT'S BEEN FUN TYING IT IN DIFFERENT WAYS.
I KNOW WHAT YOU MEAN. I DO SOMETHING SIMILAR.
FOR ME, IT'S THIS.
슥
I CHANGE THEM UP EVERY WEEK AND IT'S PRETTY FUN.

I GET IT. WE ALL NEED A LITTLE SOMETHING.
WOW. PLEASE DO MY NAILS.
MAYBE, IT'S SOMETHING LIKE THIS —IT FEELS LIKE I'M GIVING MYSELF SOME LOVE.
WHOAAA
FOR ME IT'S ABOUT...
SCRUBBING HARD IN THE SHOWER TO REALLY EXFOLIATE. THEN I LIKE TO APPLY SOME NICE BODY LOTION.
SELF LOVE IS DIFFERENT FOR EVERY PERSON.
I'M GIVING MYSELF A LITTLE LOVE RIGHT NOW BY EATING THIS CAKE!

AH, I JUST REMEMBERED THERE'S SOMETHING I NEED TO BUY.
Let's go to the grocery store.
마트
Mart
BIG SALE !!
Beep
THIS IS OUT OF THE BLUE?
CURRY POWDER?
CURRY POWDER
UM...
LET'S SAY IT'S A WAY OF GIVING MYSELF SOME LOVE.
?

How To Tie Hair Without A Hair Tie

YES, OKAY.
UNDERSTOOD.
I'LL SEND THE EMAIL.
PLEASE LET ME KNOW IF THERE'S ANYTHING THAT NEEDS TO BE ADJUSTED.
YOU AS WELL.

Toss
Toss
Whomp
I DON'T WANT TO DIE LIKE THIS BUT I FEEL DEAD TIRED.

I'M ALSO HUNGRY... BUT MAYBE I'LL TAKE A NAP FIRST.
BUZZ
BUZZZ BUZZZ
RUSTLE
...HELLO?
....YEAH.
NO, I JUST ENDED.
...RIGHT NOW?

SIGH...I WANTED TO SLEEP.
Life is so hard.
I want to give up on everything.
But she's my friend, and if this is what she's posting on social media, I really can't ignore her call.
HOW ABOUT TOMORROW...
...NEVER MIND. NO, YEAH I'LL HEAD OUT NOW. JUST GIVE ME TEN MINUTES.
HM
Gloom

rustle
NO CHOICE.
LET'S JUST PUT SOMETHING ON AND GO MEET HER.
헤어
수선

SORRY, SORRY
I'M A LITTLE LATE, HUH?
shake, shake
IT'S ALRIGHT...
...I SMELL ALCOHOL.
IT LOOKS LIKE YOU ALREADY HAD ONE WITHOUT ME.
OKAY, LET'S DRINK.
YEAH. YOU WANT ANOTHER ONE?
TODAY I JUST REALLY WANT TO DRINK.
파출부
이비인후과
노래방
GOT IT, GOT IT.

...SO, WHAT'S UP WITH YOU THESE DAYS-
ACK!
DIP
HUH?
sway, sway
YOU ALRIGHT?
GEEZ, THIS WON'T DO.

How To Tie Hair Without A Hair Tie

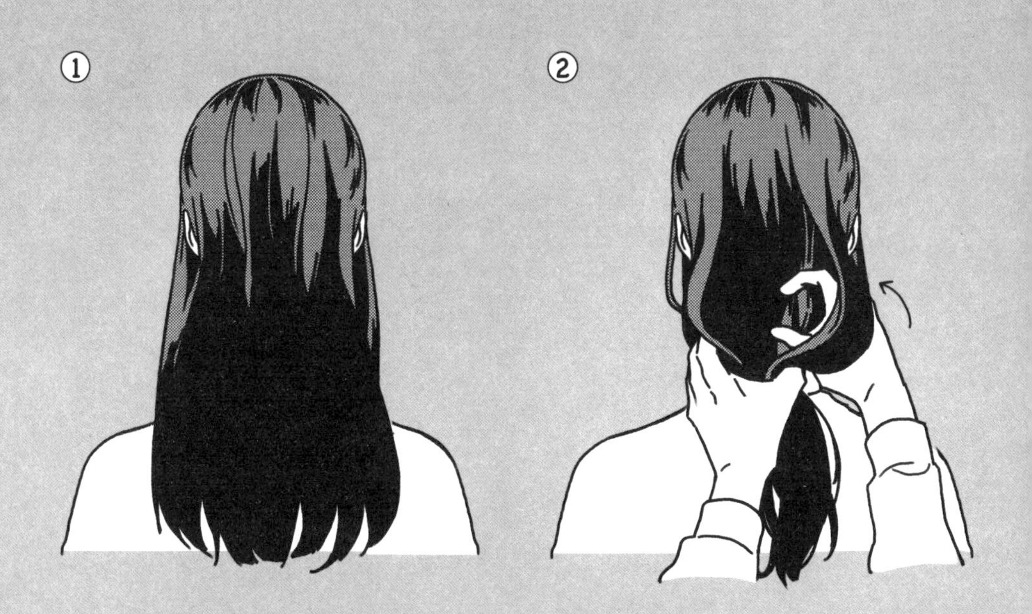

Gather the hair and make it neat.

Take all the hair into one hand, then above it put your thumb and index finger through the hair to creat an opening.

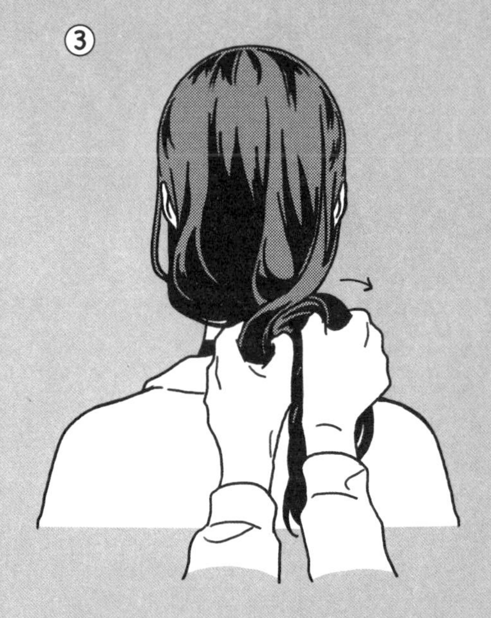

Pull the remaining hair through the opening you created.

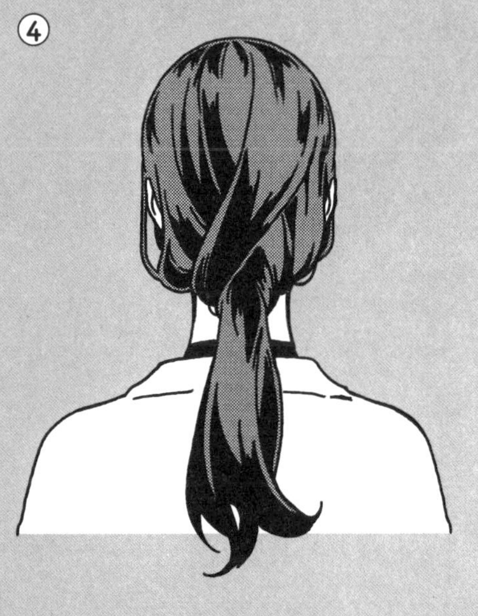

If you feel it's too loose, repeat the process two or three times.

DID YOU SOBER UP A LITTLE BIT? ARE YOU OKAY?
blink
LET'S STOP HERE AND HEAD HOME.
NO, I'M FINE. I'M SOBER. THANKS.
THAT'S USUALLY WHAT DRUNK PEOPLE SAY.
......
FINE, LET'S SIT HERE A WHILE LONGER UNTIL YOU SOBER UP A BIT.
YEAH... I'M NOT DRUNK.
rattle
SURE, SURE. ... ARE YOU HAVING A HARD TIME LATELY? DID SOMETHING HAPPEN?

IF YOU DON'T WANT TO TALK ABOUT IT, YOU DON'T HAVE TO. LIFE'S DIFFICULT, HUH?
YEAH. AND IT'S NO FUN.
glug, glug
chug
BEING AROUND PEOPLE IS TIRING,
BEING ALONE IS LONELY.
ONCE THE SADNESS CREEPS IN,
I CAN ONLY BE SAD, I CAN'T DO ANYTHING ELSE.

nods
RATTLE
ACK.
I dozed off...
HOLD ON, HOLD ON A MINUTE.
Grab
LET'S STOP DRINKING. WE'RE DONE FOR TODAY!
DRINKING WHILE EXHAUSTED, THAT COULD'VE BEEN REALLY BAD.

WHY DON'T YOU SLEEP OVER AT MY PLACE TODAY? PLEASE?
초밥
酒
酒
래방
만화
술
IT'S FINE...I'M FINE. I CAN GO HOME BY MYSELF. I'M NOT DRUNK.
HEY, IT'S A SCARY WORLD WHERE GIRLS CAN'T EVEN GO TO THE BATHROOM BY THEMSELVES.
DO YOU THINK I'LL BE ABLE TO SLEEP COMFORTABLY AFTER SENDING YOU HOME ALONE?
......
BUT YOU'RE TAKING THE FLOOR, GOT IT?
......OKAY.
JB
래방
cof
...I'M KIDDING. YOU CAN HAVE THE BED.

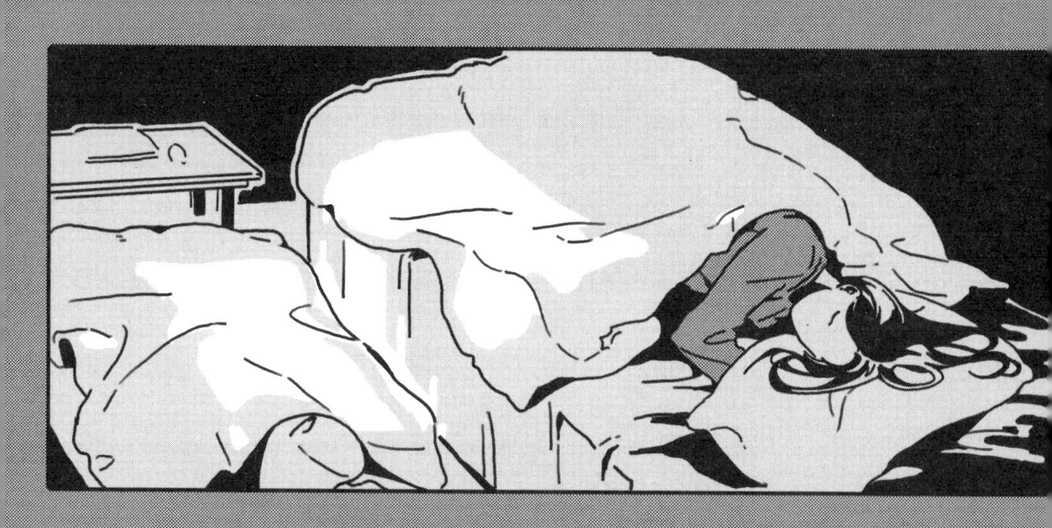

Pant, pant

IT'S ANOTHER DREAM WHERE I'M BEING CHASED.
BUT I DON'T WANT TO RUN...
HEY, IT'S TIME TO EAT.
HUH?

WHAT'S THIS? CURRY? DID YOU MAKE IT?
YEAH. IT'S HANGOVER CURRY.
WHATEVER WE HAVE TO DO, LET'S START BY SLEEPING WELL AND EATING WELL. THIS ISN'T ANY ORDINARY CURRY, YOU KNOW?
......
...I LIKE MIXING MY CURRY COMPLETELY WITH MY RICE.
FOR REAL? I'M ON THE SIDE OF SCOOPING UP THE CURRY AND EATING IT SEPARATELY WITH THE RICE.
OH,
ALSO COULD YOU TIE MY HAIR AGAIN?
YES MA'AM.

How To Tie Your Hair Using A Scarf

Hello. I am a fairy.
You guys probably don't know it, but according to the rules of the fairy realm, there's one of us in every household.
Our main job is to borrow things that are around our own size.
?
Once the owner buys the same item again, we put the other one back where it belongs.
Why in the world would we do such a thing?
TO REMIND YOU THAT
YOU HAVE TO CLEAN YOUR ROOM, DAMN IT.

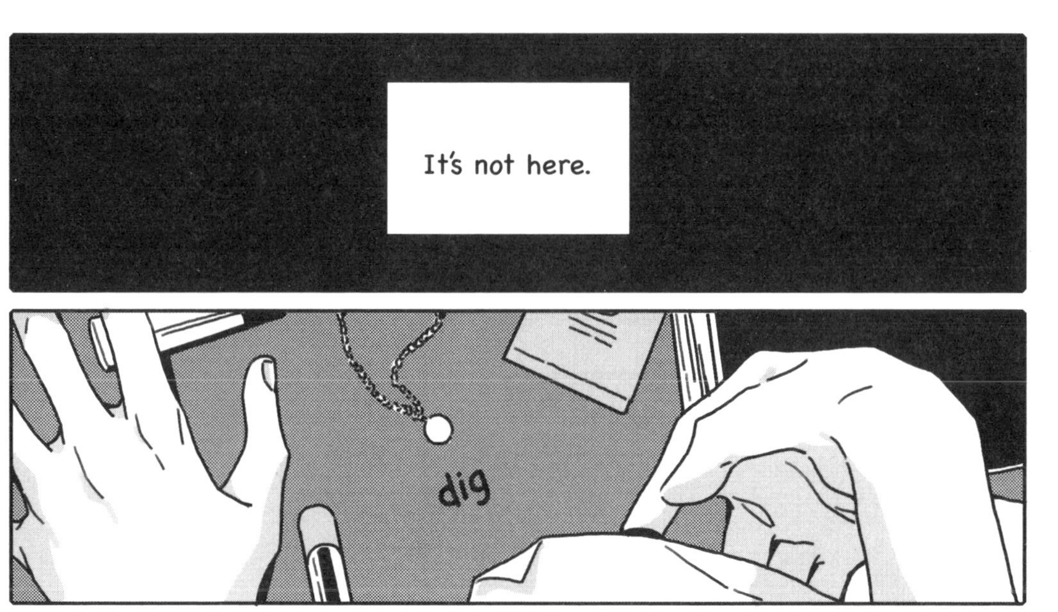

I had so many hair ties—how could they all have disappeared?

I left my wallet at home.

Today is a day when I have a lot of errands to run. I need to stop by places I have to stop at, and get back after buying things I need to buy. It's an important day.

I left my ID at home.

clatter
GASP.
rattle
09:00 ~16:00
……………
WHY DOES THE BANK CLOSE SO EARLY...DO I NEED TO COME BACK AGAIN TOMORROW.
OH WELL... I'LL STOP BY THE DMV AND BUY SOMETHING DELICIOUS FOR DINNER BEFORE GOING HOME.

구청
rattle
WHY DOES EVERYWHERE CLOSE SO EARLY? MY DAY IS JUST STARTING.
HAHA, WHAT A NICE WALK FOR NOTHING.
I'M PISSED....
NO. THERE WAS A RESTAURANT NEARBY I'VE BEEN WANTING TO TRY. EVERYTHING'S TURNED OUT FOR THE BEST.

It feels like the entire world hates me.

I'M SORRY, MISS.
WE'RE ALL BOOKED FOR TONIGHT. LET ME HELP YOU MAKE AN APPOINTMENT FOR ANOTHER TIME.
AH, UM, NEVER MIND.
I'M FINE. THANK YOU.
PHEW.
plop.
IF I CUT IT NOW, I WOULD DEFINITELY REGRET IT. RIGHT?

Step...
LET'S START BY DOING WHAT I CAN, ONE STEP AT A TIME.
HAIRPONY
HAIRPONY
HAIRPONY
WOULD YOU LIKE TO GIFT WRAP IT?
NO, I'LL TAKE IT AS IS, PLEASE!
정리함
OH,
COULD I ALSO HAVE ONE OF THOSE?
OF COURSE.

How To Tie Your Hair Using A Scarf

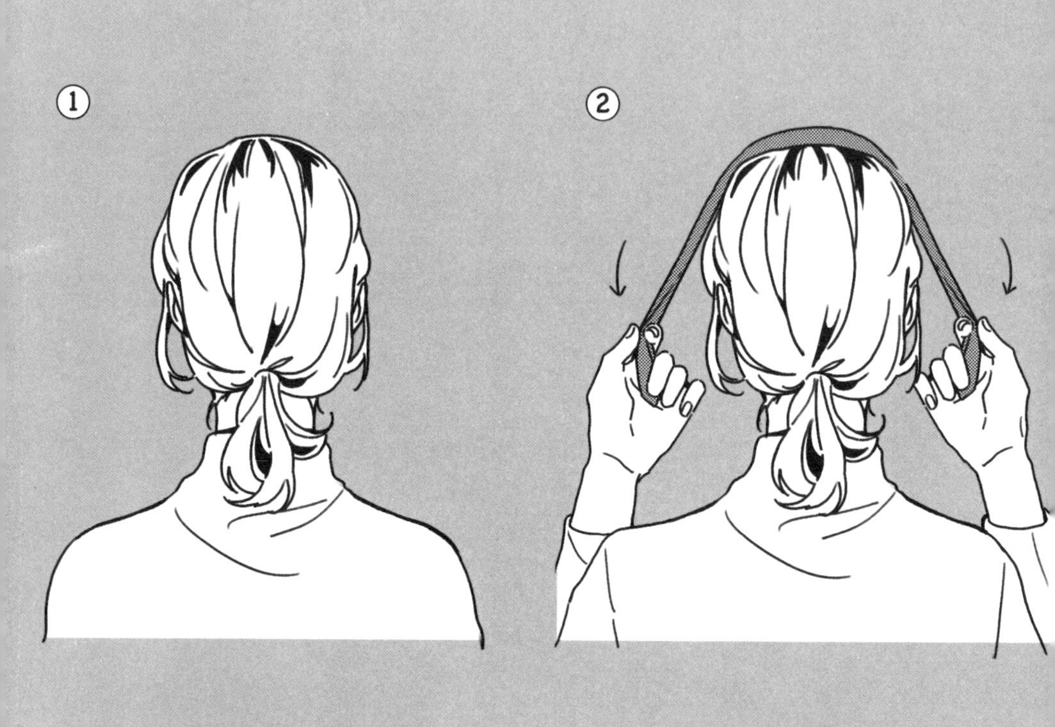

Tie your hair in a low ponytail. When wearing a headband, it's good to pay attention to the volume of the hair around your face.

After tying your hair, place the headband on your head.

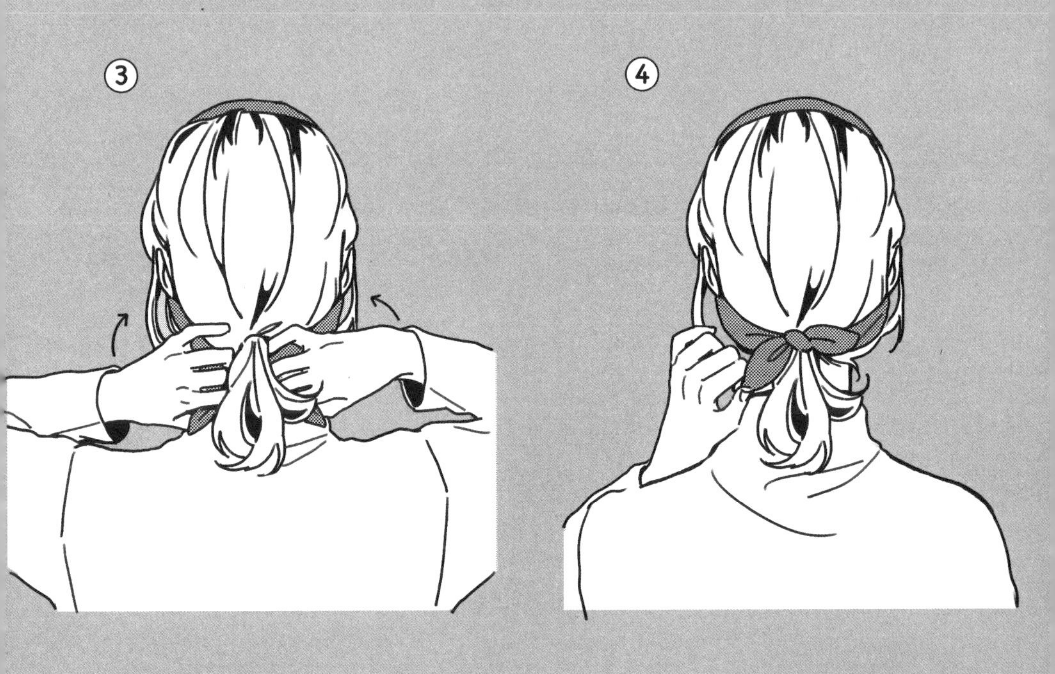

Behind the low ponytail, cross the ends of the scarf in an x-shape.

Wrap the ends around the ponytail and tie it in a bow or knot. Pull out some front pieces to make it look more natural.

AH, MUCH BETTER.
heavy
AS SOON AS I GET HOME, I'M GOING TO TIDY UP AND THEN DO A DEEP CLEAN ON THE WEEKEND.
WOMAN
WOMAN
I'LL TAKE CARE OF THE ERRANDS TOMORROW AND THE DAY AFTER...

Heehee. It looks like there was some progress made.
I'll return this to you. Leaving it under the pillow should be good.
Is the house fairy's job done now, you ask?
*Messiness cycle usually repeats bi-weekly, or monthly
Don't worry. After a couple months—no, a couple weeks—I'll have to step in again.
So, see you next time! Bye!

chirp chirp
WHY IS THIS HERE?

How To Tie Your Hair Mom's Way

Today I'm leaving my house to go to my house.

...the one that's my real home is...they're both my real homes.

RATTLE
SINCE I'LL BE STUCK ON THE BUS ALL DAY ANYWAY, I PULLED AN ALL-NIGHTER.
I'M TIRED. I DON'T WANT TO DO ANYTHING.
BAM
EVERY HOLIDAY SEASON, I FEEL THE MIGHT OF THE HUMAN SPIRIT.
SHAAAAA

치과 의원
데리아
1588-0000
NIT 내일투어
6F

ROLL
OH.
RATTLE
hurry
YIKES.

BUS TERMINAL
MALL
THAT'S NEW TO THE NEIGHBORHOOD.
음료
잡화
코팅
체육용품
문구
OH THIS PLACE, IT'S STILL HERE.
EVERY TIME I PASS BY IT, THIS FENCE SEEMS SMALLER.

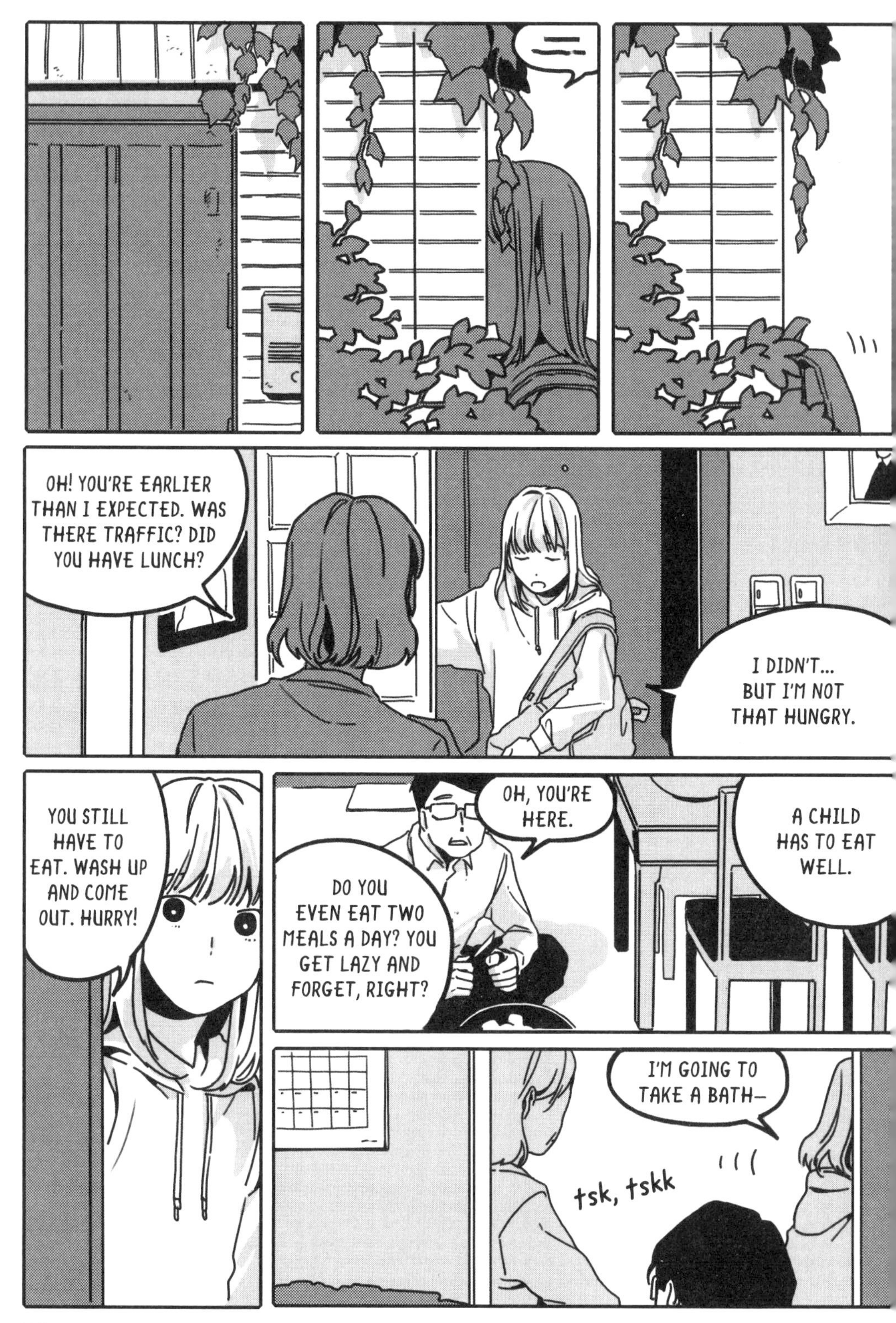

OH! YOU'RE EARLIER THAN I EXPECTED. WAS THERE TRAFFIC? DID YOU HAVE LUNCH?
I DIDN'T... BUT I'M NOT THAT HUNGRY.
YOU STILL HAVE TO EAT. WASH UP AND COME OUT. HURRY!
OH, YOU'RE HERE.
DO YOU EVEN EAT TWO MEALS A DAY? YOU GET LAZY AND FORGET, RIGHT?
A CHILD HAS TO EAT WELL.
I'M GOING TO TAKE A BATH—
tsk, tskk

splash
splish, splash
AAAAH.
I CAN'T BELIEVE I HAVE TO HEAR THEIR NAGGING FOR AT LEAST A WEEK.
tap, tap
This is still here, huh?
poke
STILL, IT'S NICE TO BE HOME.

SPLASH
click
click
RATTLE
IS THERE ANYTHING I CAN DO TO HELP?
glug, glug
OH, COULD YOU COAT THESE IN EGG?
SURE.

WHEN DID YOUR HAIR GROW OUT SO MUCH? IT'S FALLING DOWN. WON'T IT BE EASIER IF YOU TIED IT?
OH...
UM...
Drip, drip
IT'S FINE, IT'S FINE. I'LL TIE IT FOR YOU.

How To Tie Your Hair Mom's Way

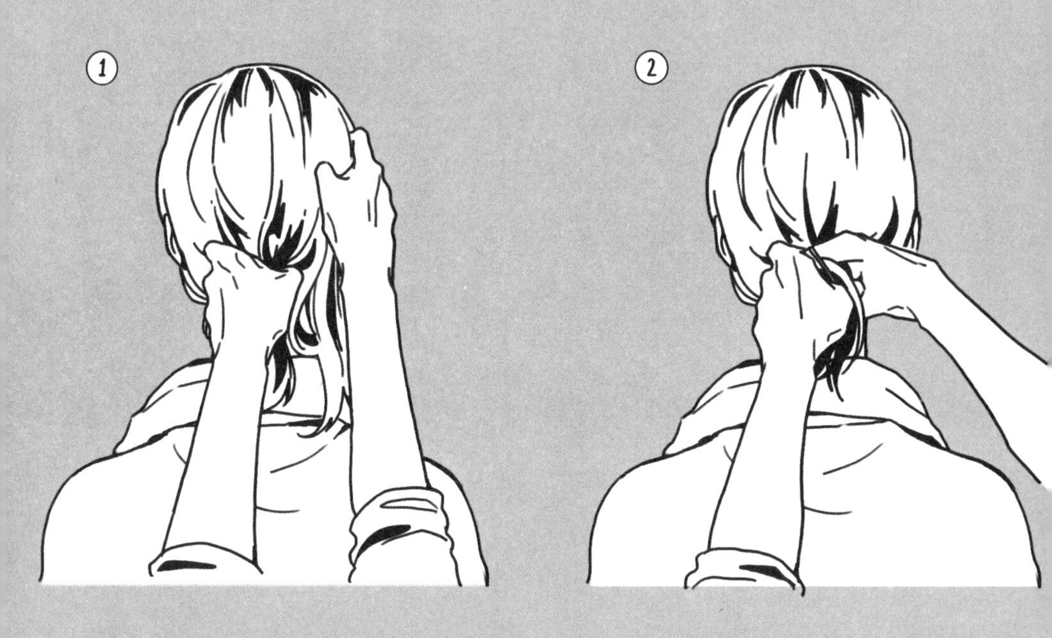

Hey, make sure to eat properly. How is it that everytime I see you, you look emaciated? Eat well and sleep well, okay? Nothing's more important than your health.

At least I don't nag you to get married. I just want you to look out for yourself.

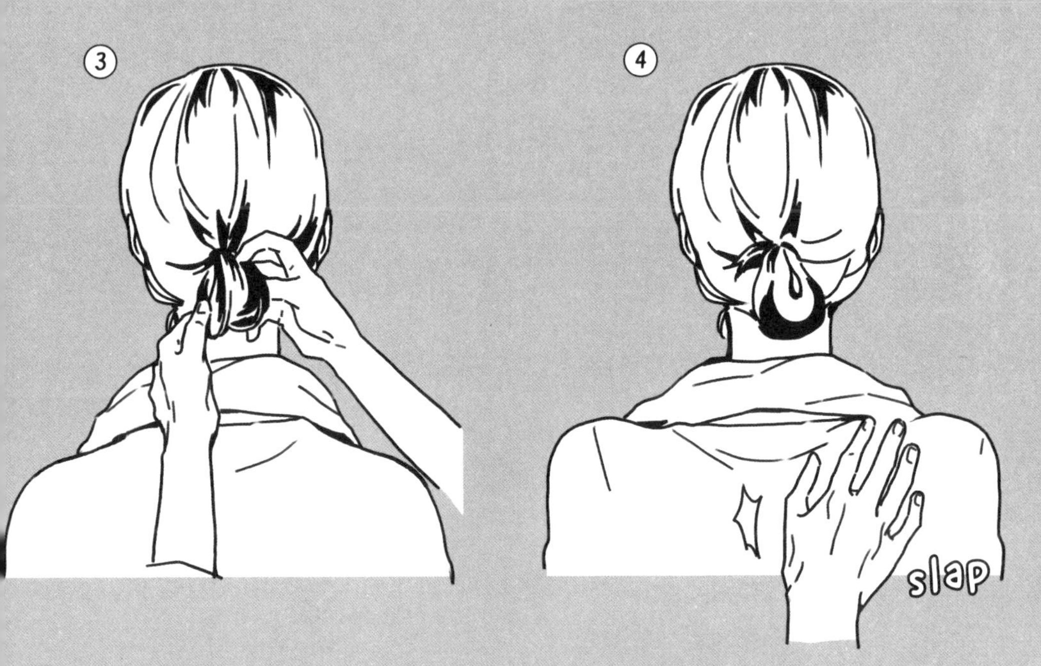

Also, try to call more often.
And if you have time, come visit.
Even if we might not show it,
we worry about you a lot.

Since you're here anyway,
get some rest. Eat a lot,
and sleep early, okay?

……
SIZZZZLE
SIZZZZLE
SIZZZZZLE

munch
OH, THESE TURNED OUT SO GOOD.
I MADE A LOT SO TAKE SOME WITH YOU WHEN YOU GO BACK.
RIGHT?
AH, I FEEL A CHILL. IT'S STARTING TO GET COLD.
SLAM
click
IT'S GOING TO BE LIKE THIS AND THEN WINTER ALL OF A SUDDEN. THERE'S REALLY NO IN-BETWEEN... BE CAREFUL OR YOU'LL CATCH A COLD.

GOODNIGHT, MOM.
GOODNIGHT, DAD.
click
SO TIRED,
SO TIRED.
HM,
I THINK IT'S BEEN ABOUT 20 YEARS SINCE MOM TIED MY HAIR.
yank
OW!
...IF YOU TIE HAIR WITH A YELLOW RUBBERBAND, IT HURTS WHEN YOU TAKE IT OUT.
HMM...MOM'S LOVE IS LIKE A YELLOW RUBBERBAND...

I DIDN'T KNOW THOSE WERE STILL STUCK UP THERE.
...WHILE I'M HOME I SHOULD EAT WELL AND SLEEP WELL AND GET SOME REST.
NO, WHEN I GO BACK TO MY HOME I SHOULD LIVE WELL.
NO, WHEN I HAVE MY OWN LAND ONE DAY...
Snore-

The Day I Returned
HANG ON. LET ME SEE IF YOU'RE FORGETTING ANYTHING.
NO, MOM...AT THIS POINT, IT'S BETTER TO FORGET THINGS.

How To Tie Your Hair In A Comfortable Bun

Somehow, I ended up cleaning out my fridge.

Then somehow, I started cleaning out my clothes...

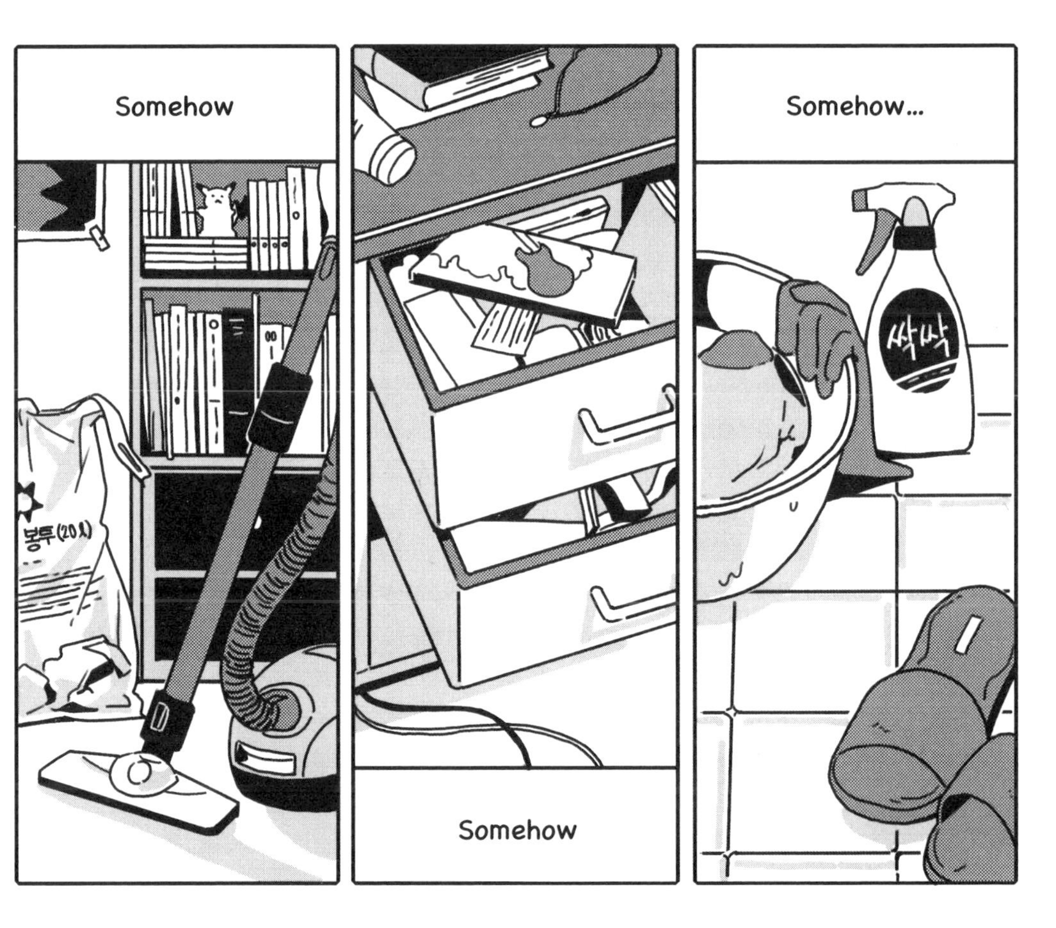

You never feel like cleaning, but once you gain momentum
a hellish chain reaction begins.

How To Tie Your Hair In A Comfortable Bun

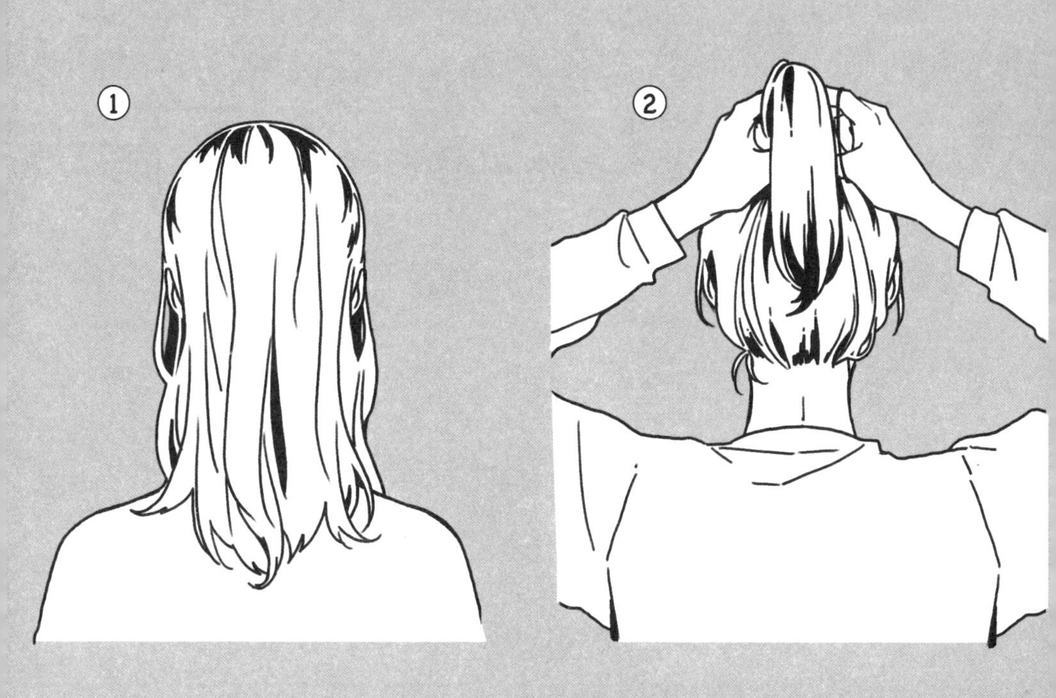

1. Brush out your hair and make it look neat. A bun is great for when you have unwashed, tangled hair.

2. Gather your hair toward the crown of your head and tie it high. One way to do it is to lean your head forward.

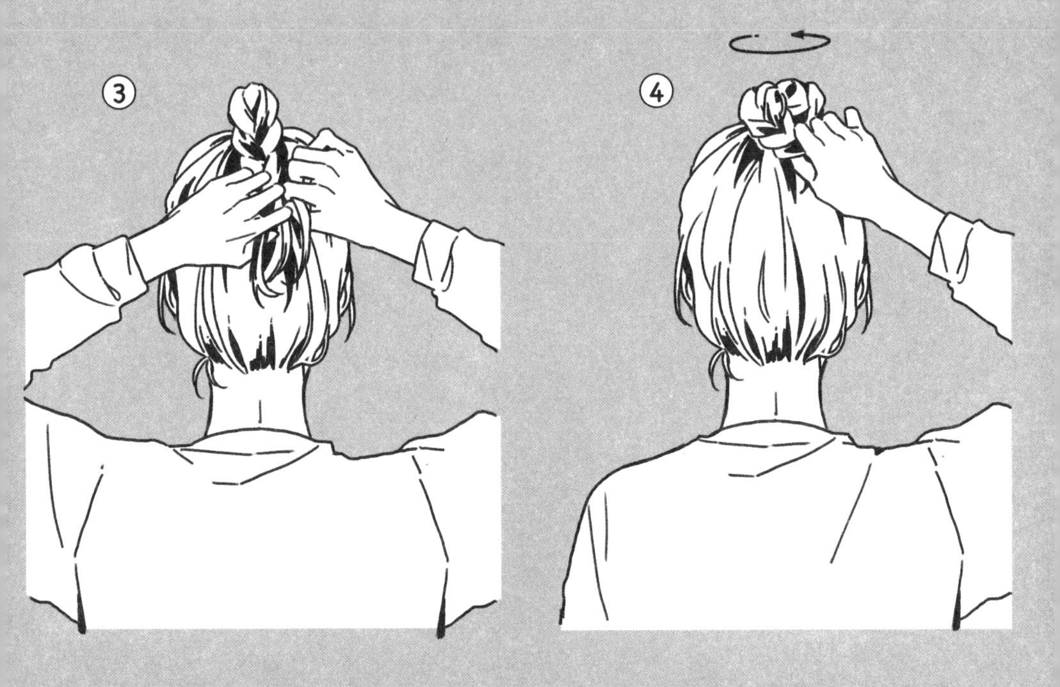

Part the high ponytail into three sections and braid them. It's alright to just braid halfway.

Just like that, roll up the hair into a bun in a counter-clockwise direction, and tie it with a second hair tie.

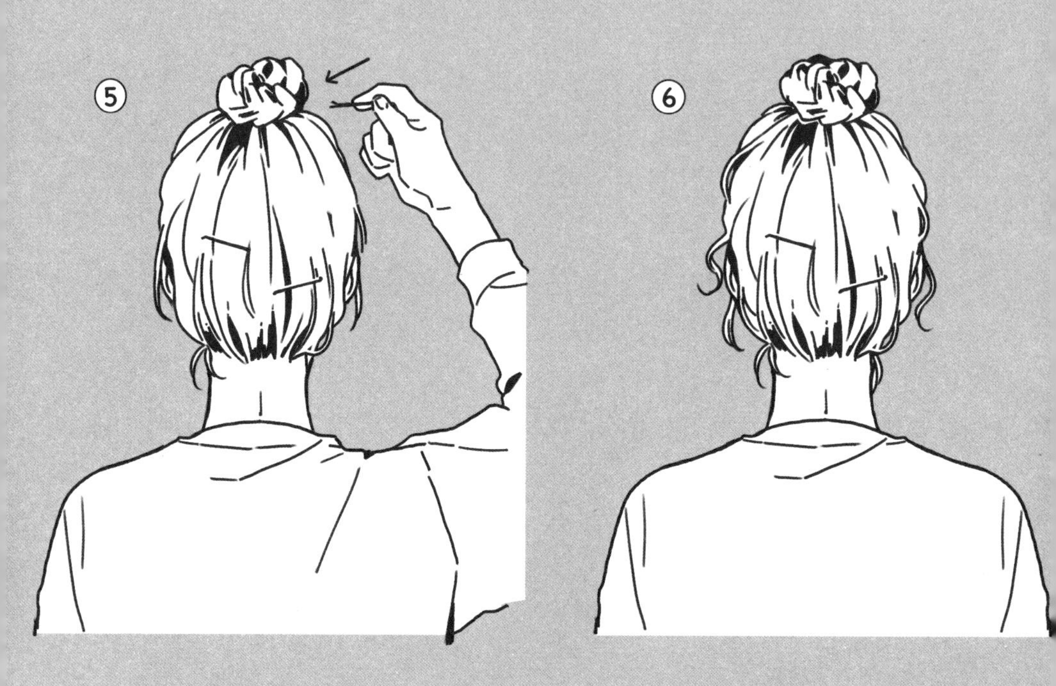

After tying with a rubber band, if there are parts sticking out, secure with a bobby pin or barrette. Do the same for any wisps or loose strands that stick out.

For the areas lacking volume, you can add slight curls to the loose strands to style it in a variety of ways.

creak
BRRR, IT'S COLD.
IT'S TOTALLY WINTER NOW.

OKAY, THEN...
우체국
WHERE SHOULD I START CLEANING?

OH MY GOSH,
I CAN'T BELIEVE THIS WAS HERE ALL ALONG. CRAZY. I JUST BOUGHT A NEW ONE.
쓰레기봉투
쓰레기봉투
쓰레기봉투
HAHA, THAT'S HILARIOUS. IT'S FROM 2007. I ONLY WROTE ON THREE PAGES AND THEN STOPPED.
……
OH WAIT, I WAS IN THE MIDDLE OF CLEANING.

HUH.
HUH. THIS...SHE MUST HAVE LEFT IT WHEN SHE VISITED.
NEXT TIME, I SEE HER I'LL GIVE IT TO HER. FOR NOW, INTO THE JEWELRY ORGANIZER...
HUH?
dig
dig
WHAT'S GOING ON? WHERE'S THE OTHER EARRING? WHERE DID I LEAVE IT?
AW, I REALLY LIKE THIS PAIR! DID I DROP IT SOMEWHERE WHILE I WAS CLEANING?

SIGH.
Oh well.
stuffed
쓰레기
stuffed
flip
WHY DO WE HUMANS GENERATE SO MUCH WASTE?
One, two...
쓰레기
rip
rip

riiip
riiip
riiip
POP
ping
CLATTER
BAM
ROLLL

....WHAT JUST HAPPENED.
STUFF THE THE BAGS FULL TO TRY TO SAVE A FEW CENTS, AND LOOK WHAT HAPPENS.
SIGH...
Grab
I'M PATHETIC. SO PATHETIC.
WHY AM I ALWAYS LIKE THIS?
Grab

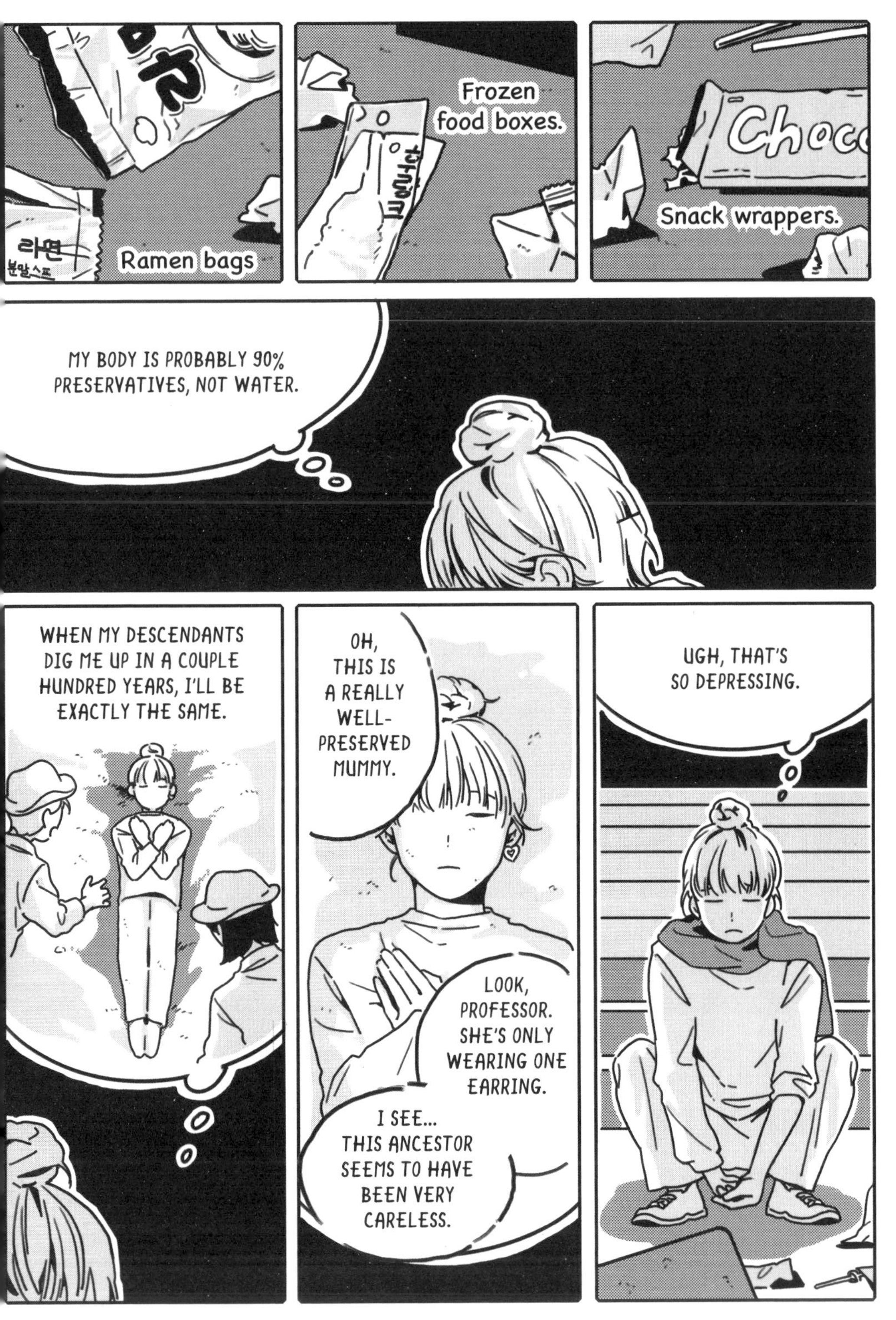

Ramen bags
라면
분말스프
Frozen food boxes.
Snack wrappers.
MY BODY IS PROBABLY 90% PRESERVATIVES, NOT WATER.
WHEN MY DESCENDANTS DIG ME UP IN A COUPLE HUNDRED YEARS, I'LL BE EXACTLY THE SAME.
OH, THIS IS A REALLY WELL-PRESERVED MUMMY.
LOOK, PROFESSOR. SHE'S ONLY WEARING ONE EARRING.
I SEE... THIS ANCESTOR SEEMS TO HAVE BEEN VERY CARELESS.
UGH, THAT'S SO DEPRESSING.

BUS TICKET.
Grab
I WANT TO GO HOME. I WANT TO EAT MY MOM'S COOKING.
OH, A CORNDOG STICK.
IT WAS YOU!
YOU'RE THE CULPRIT THAT RIPPED THE TRASH BAG TO SHREDS!
WHAT THIS?
IT'S THE OTHER EARRING!
IT MUST'VE FALLEN INTO THE TRASH BIN.
WHAT A RELIEF! I ALMOST THREW IT AWAY. THANK GOD, THANK GOD.

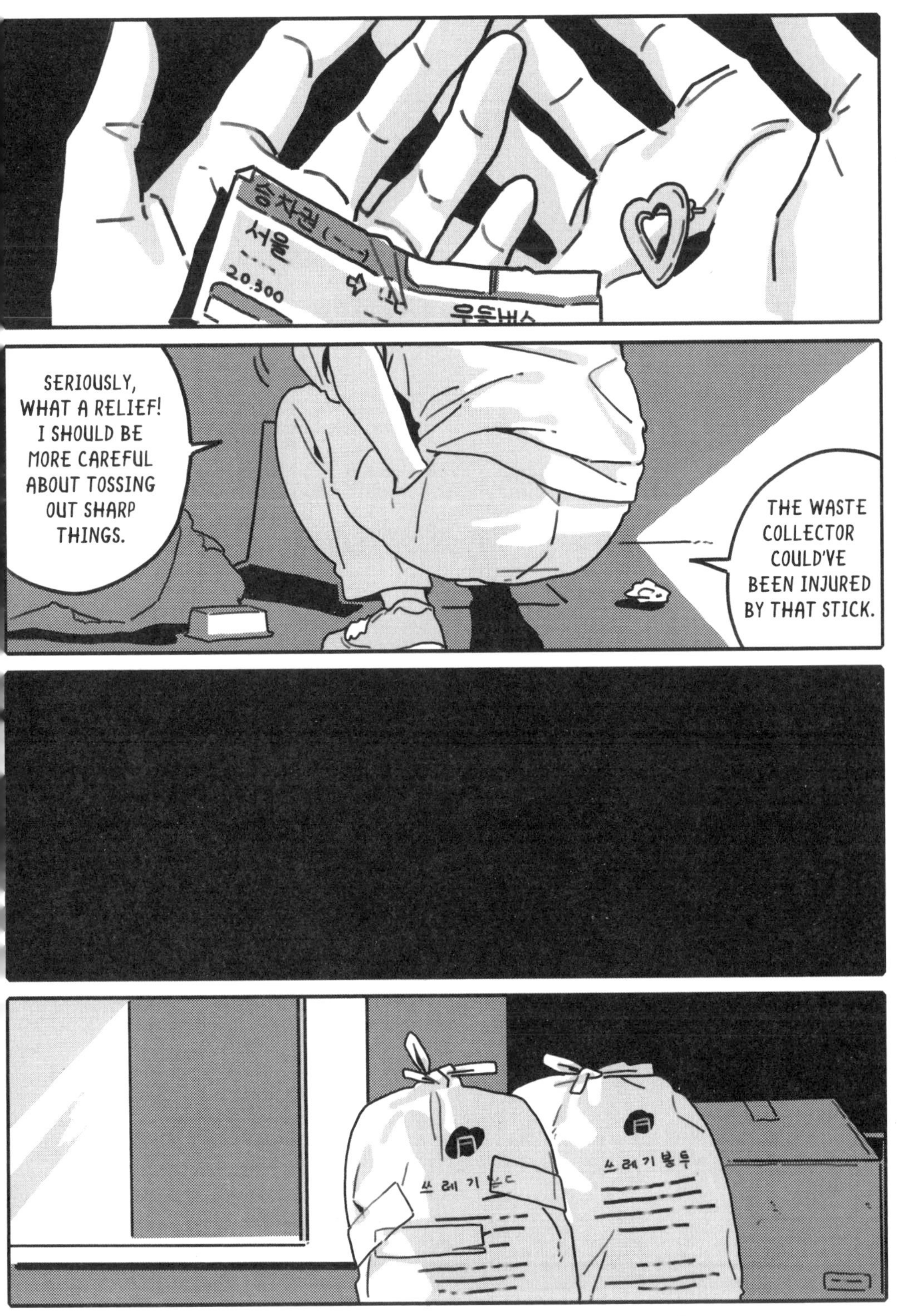
승차권
서울
20.300
SERIOUSLY, WHAT A RELIEF! I SHOULD BE MORE CAREFUL ABOUT TOSSING OUT SHARP THINGS.
THE WASTE COLLECTOR COULD'VE BEEN INJURED BY THAT STICK.
쓰레기봉투

ring
bubble
bubble
ring
DELICIOUS! LEFTOVER STEW IS THE BEST.
HELLO?
HI, MOM.
WERE YOU SLEEPING? YEAH. JUST BECAUSE.
YEAH, I'M DOING GREAT ON MY OWN.
TODAY?.... I CLEANED AND TOOK A SHOWER. NOW, I'M MAKING STEW FROM THE CHUSEOK HOLIDAY LEFTOVERS. YEAH? OH RIGHT, NEXT MONTH...

How To Tie A Ponytail For Long Hair

nods
zzzz
Gasp
DID YOU PULL AN ALL-NIGHTER AGAIN THINKING YOU'LL SLEEP IN THE CAR?
NO... I SLEPT BUT I FELL ASLEEP KIND OF LATE.
WERE YOU UNABLE TO SLEEP BECAUSE YOU WERE EXCITED FOR THE TRIP? HAHA.
......
IT'S TRUE, I WAS EXCITED.
Stand clear of the closing doors.
chuga, chuga zoom
HEY, WE HAVE TO GET OFF, GET OFF.
Ack

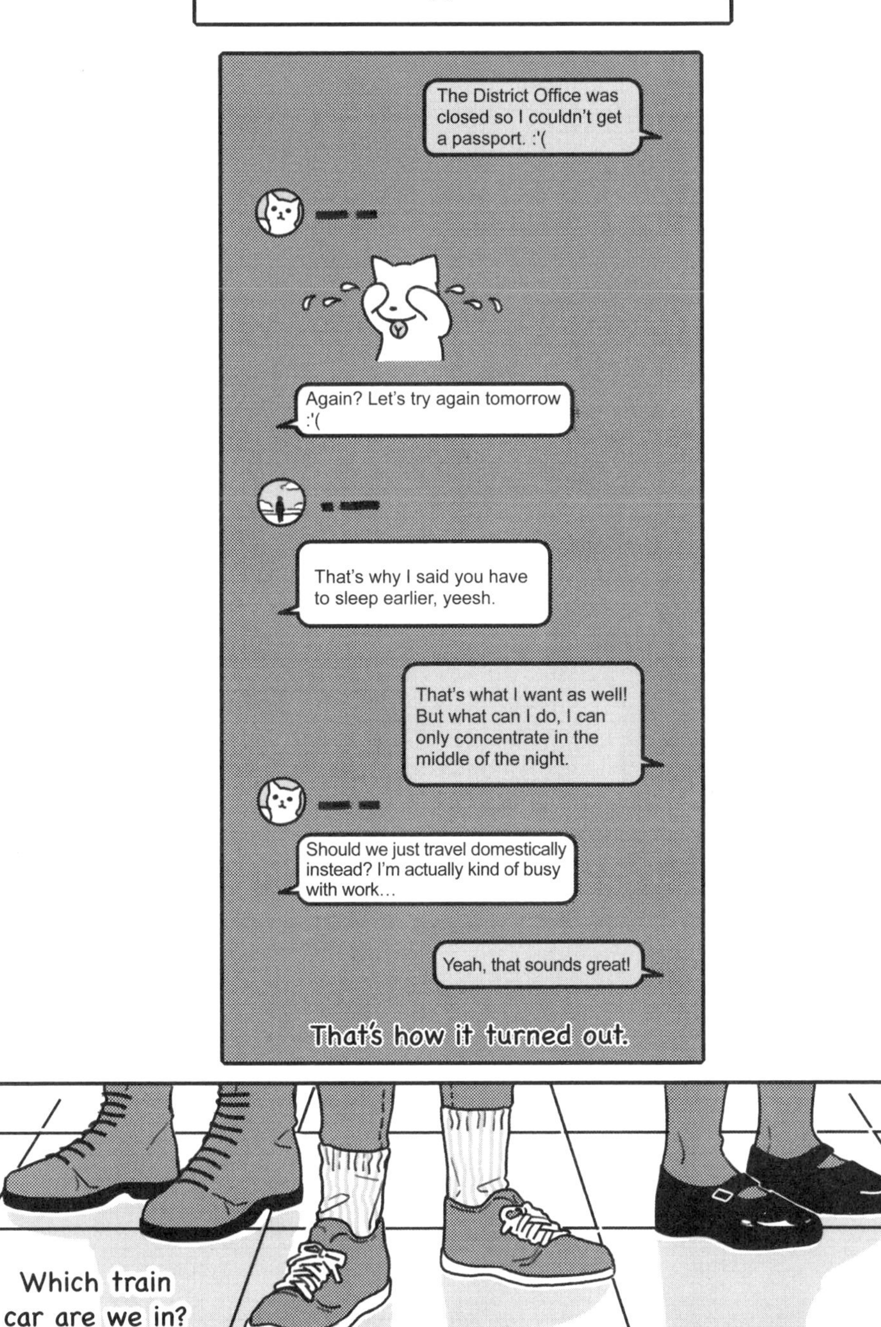
What happened was...
The District Office was closed so I couldn't get a passport. :'(
Again? Let's try again tomorrow :'(
That's why I said you have to sleep earlier, yeesh.
That's what I want as well! But what can I do, I can only concentrate in the middle of the night.
Should we just travel domestically instead? I'm actually kind of busy with work…
Yeah, that sounds great!
That's how it turned out.
Which train car are we in? Check the ticket.

It's the end of the year,
and it's winter
so we decided to go see the
sunrise over the winter sea.
bounce
bounce

EVERYONE'S READY, RIGHT?
OF COURSE.
LET'S GO, ONE
TWO,
포타칩
Original
THREE!
NOT AGAIN?
Pop
팡
YOU GOTTA GO WITH THE CLASSIC, ORIGINAL FLAVOR FOR POTATO CHIPS.
I LIKE SOUR CREAM AND ONION.
YOU'RE BOTH WRONG. FOR SNACKS, ANYTHING WITH CHOCOLATE IS THE BEST, OKAY?

For me it didn't matter where we were going on our trip. The point was to go somewhere far, far away and stay a while before coming back.

For a moment, we're placing everything we're used to at a great distance. Are we just justifying an escape from reality?

OH.
SORRY, GIVE ME A SECOND.
Manager
SHE'S ON VACATION AND THEY'RE STILL CALLING HER.
THAT'S REALLY PROBLEMATIC.
YES, HELLO? YES, YES.
NO, IT'S NOT IN THAT FOLDER BUT THE SEAGULL FOLDER. NOT THE PIGEON FOLDER...
갈매기
I WAS STILL WORKING ON IT SO I HAVEN'T HAD TIME TO INCORPORATE THE CHANGES. YES, THAT'S THE FILE. YES, ALRIGHT, UNDERSTOOD.
SORRY, SORRY!
Of course, even justified escapes aren't easy to pull off.

KORAIL
WHOAAA, MY BUTT HURTS. EVEN JUST SITTING IS HARD WORK.
BUT STILL, IT'S NICE TO SMELL THE SEA AIR. RIGHT?
bzzzzzz
...IT'S OKAY IF YOU GO ANSWER THE PHONE!
WE'LL BE LOOKING AROUND AT THE SEA.
YEAH, YEAH, DON'T WORRY ABOUT IT.
Ultimately, it's only a momentary escape.
......
WHEN I RETURN, I'LL BE BACK TO DEADLINES...
To prepare for the day when we eventually have to return. The things we left behind keep poking at our hearts.
I NEED TO MAKE SURE TO CALL THE CLIENT IN ADVANCE.

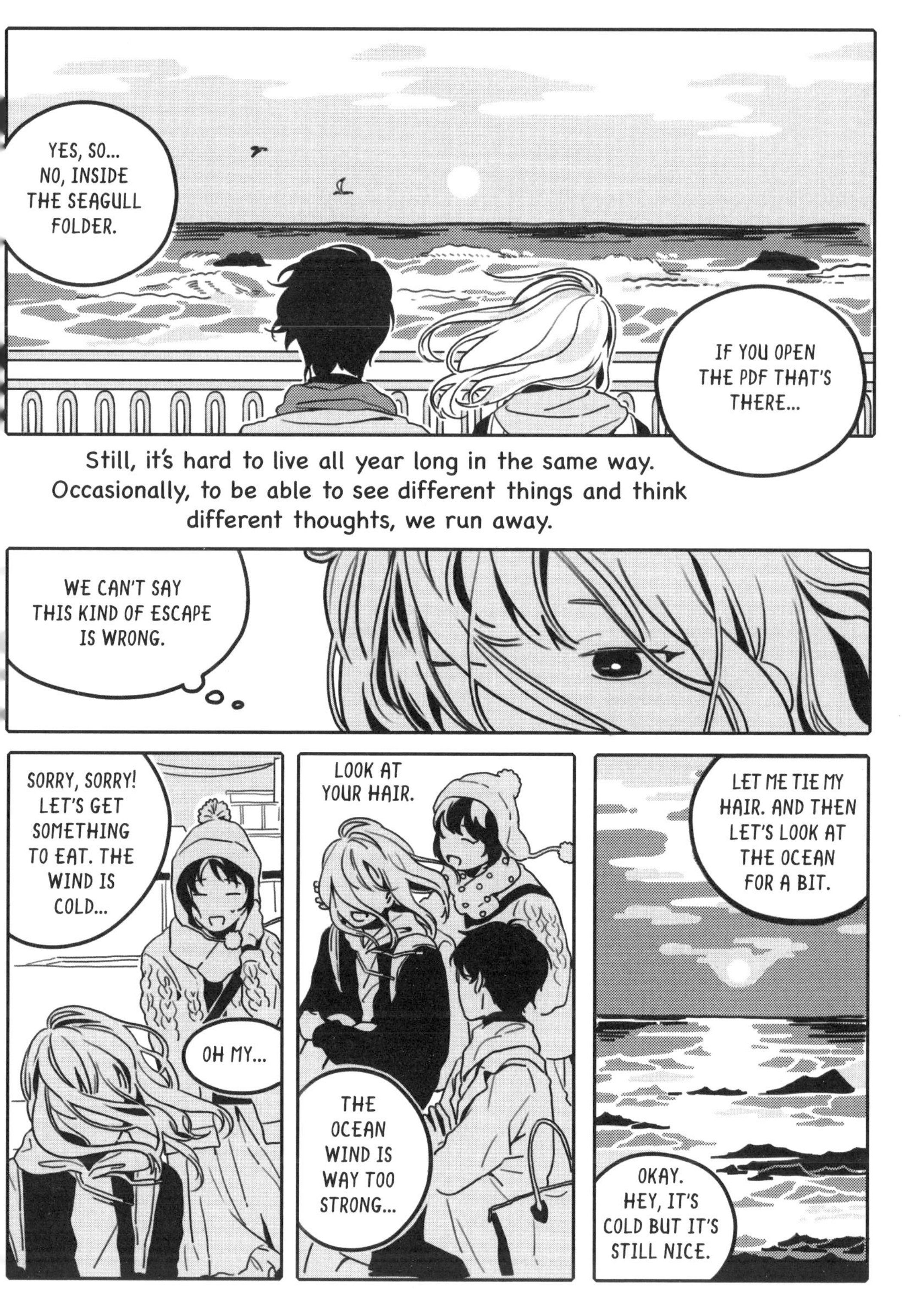

YES, SO... NO, INSIDE THE SEAGULL FOLDER.
IF YOU OPEN THE PDF THAT'S THERE...
Still, it's hard to live all year long in the same way. Occasionally, to be able to see different things and think different thoughts, we run away.
WE CAN'T SAY THIS KIND OF ESCAPE IS WRONG.
SORRY, SORRY! LET'S GET SOMETHING TO EAT. THE WIND IS COLD...
OH MY...
LOOK AT YOUR HAIR.
THE OCEAN WIND IS WAY TOO STRONG...
LET ME TIE MY HAIR. AND THEN LET'S LOOK AT THE OCEAN FOR A BIT.
OKAY. HEY, IT'S COLD BUT IT'S STILL NICE.

How To Tie A Ponytail For Long Hair

Position where you want to tie your hair, and use your fingers as a brush to draw a parabola to gather the hair, then tie it together.

Split the ponytail in two sections, top and bottom, and pull to add volume to the hair.

Grab a strand of hair from the ponytail, and wrap around the hair tie and secure with a bobby pin.

4

If you place a tiny claw clip right under the ponytail, it will prevent the ponytail from drooping down from the weight of the hair. Finish up by fixing the volume at the crown and on the back of the head, and tucking away the stray hairs using a bobby pin.

WE'RE GETTING KNIFE-CUT NOODLES IN BROTH FOR DINNER, RIGHT?
YEAH, IT'S THE PERFECT WEATHER FOR NOODLES.
LET'S GO, LET'S GO. I'M STARVING...
칼국수
써비스

...IS EVERYTHING ALRIGHT AT WORK?
YEAH. THEY WON'T BE CALLING ANYMORE. PROBABLY...
Bzzzzzz
FAMOUS LAST WORDS.

MAYBE IT'S IMPOSSIBLE TO JUST LIGHTLY BRUSH ASIDE CERTAIN PROBLEMS THAT WILL CHASE YOU TO THE ENDS OF THE EARTH.
BUT AT THIS RATE, I'M GOING TO BE TRIGGERED EVERY TIME I HEAR "SEAGULL FOLDER".
PHEW...
Call Ended
00:07:36
click
...LET'S STOP TALKING ABOUT THE FOLDER AND GO SEE THE REAL THING AFTER WE FINISH EATING.
HUH?

HM...
Bite
Ack!
HM... PERHAPS THE PINNACLE OF SNACKS ARE SHRIMP CHIPS, THEY'RE EVEN POPULAR WITH BIRDS.
YOU MIGHT BE RIGHT.
WHOA, REAL SEAGULLS ARE BIGGER AND SCARIER THAN I THOUGHT.
STILL, WHEN YOU SEE THEM GATHERED AROUND LIKE THAT, THEY'RE KIND OF CUTE, HUH?
YEAH, I GUESS THAT'S TRUE.

……
munch
press
Power Off
Airplane Mode
Restart
OH, YOU'RE GOING TO TURN IT OFF? WHAT ABOUT WORK?
YEAH, IT SHOULD BE OKAY. I ALREADY DID ALL I CAN... AND AS FOR SEAGULLS, I'M HAPPY WITH THE ONES THAT ARE IN FRONT OF ME.
GREAT! LET'S LOOK AROUND A BIT MORE AND HEAD TO OUR DIGS BEFORE THE SUN SETS.
SHOULD WE BUY SOME SNACKS AND BEERS ON THE WAY?
HECK YEAH!

How To Do A French Fishtail Braid

……
11:46 AM
AS EXPECTED...
...IT'S NOT LIKE THE SUN DOESN'T RISE EVERY MORNING.
TRUE, I ACTUALLY SEE THE SUN RISE EVERY DAY. BECAUSE I USUALLY STAY UP ALL NIGHT.
I DON'T THINK I'VE EVER GONE SOMEWHERE WITH THE AIM OF SEEING THE SUNRISE AND SUCCEEDED... MAYBE ONCE WHEN I WAS YOUNG AND I WENT WITH MY PARENTS.
IT'S IMPOSSIBLE TO DO UNLESS THERE'S AN ADULT WHO'LL WAKE US UP.
...WHEN WILL WE BECOME ADULTS?

SHAMPOO
...?
prick
SPLAH
prick
????
ouch, ouch
HEY, I NEED TO GO BADLY. IF YOU'RE DONE WASHING, COULD YOU HURRY UP AND COME OUT?
?? OKAY...

WHOSE STRAIGHTENER IS THIS? CAN I USE IT?
OF COURSE...
I THINK I LEFT MY CONCEALER AT HOME.
YOU CAN USE MINE. IT'S IN THE MAKEUP POUCH.
HM....
Messy
OOF, THE STATIC ELECTRICITY IS INSANE.
HOW ARE YOU EVEN SUPPOSED TO STYLE YOUR HAIR WHEN YOU WEAR A SCARF? IT LOOKS WEIRD IF I TUCK IT IN AND IT LOOKS WEIRD IF I PULL IT OUT.
IT'LL BE BETTER IF I TIE IT.

First, brush out the hair according to grain, gather the hair at the top and using the hair tie...

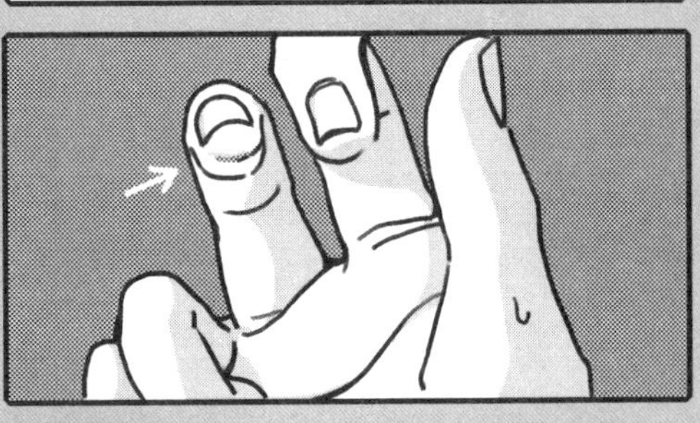

How To Do A French Fishtail Braid

Brush out your hair and divide the hair into two sections. Divide the two sections in half again so you have four strands in total.

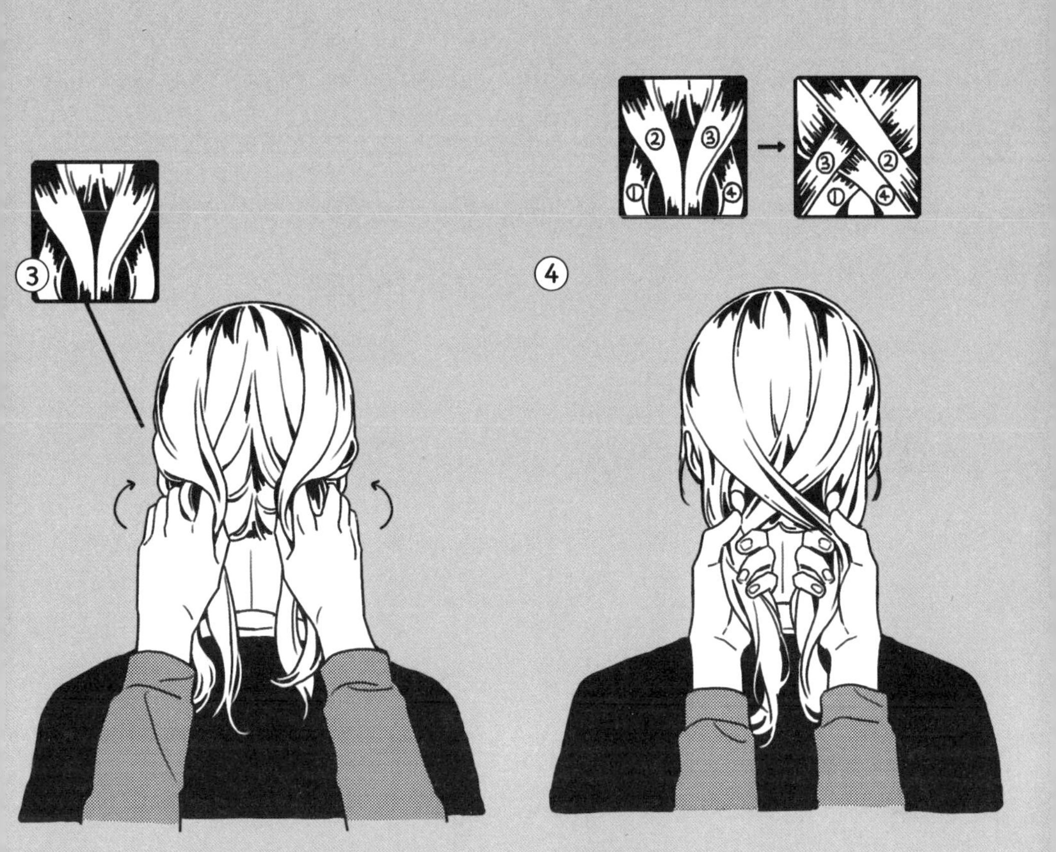

From the four strands, take the two outermost pieces from both sides and bring them to the middle.

Calling the four strands in order as 1, 2, 3, 4, combine strands 1 and 3 together, and strands 2 and 4 together to have two sections again.

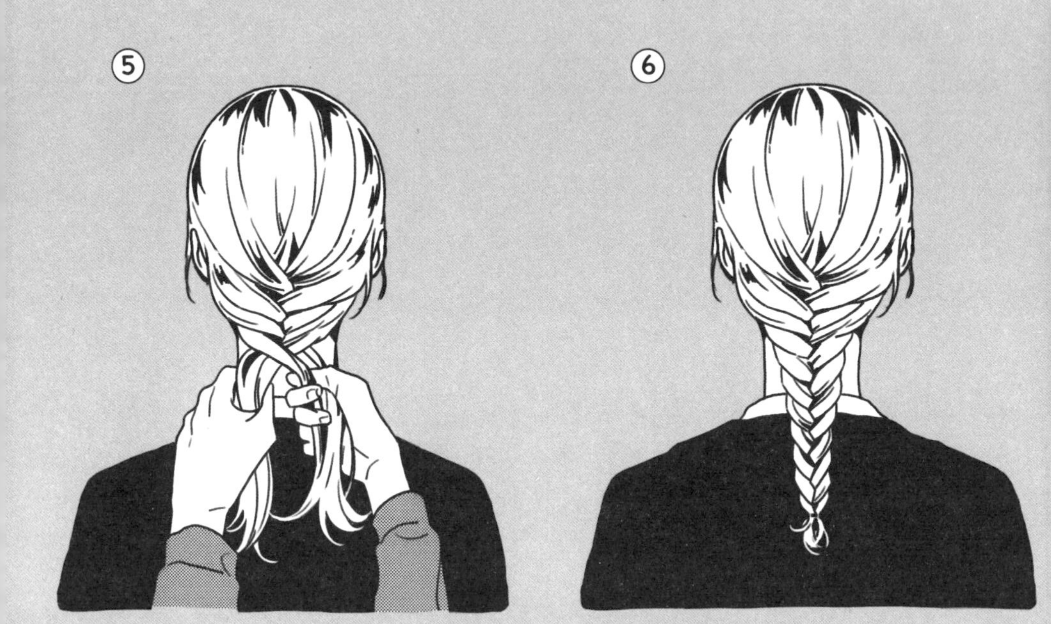

Again, take the two sections and divide in half to create four strands. And repeat the process of taking the outermost pieces and pulling them inward to combine into two sections.

The tighter you make the braid, and the smaller the pieces you use, the prettier the braid will be. For stray hairs on the side, use a hair iron to curl it slightly to finish.

IT LOOKS SO CUTE. THANKS!
I HAVE A BAND-AID. DO YOU WANT IT?
NAH, IT'S OKAY. IT'S JUST A LITTLE CUT.
NOW THAT THAT'S ALL DONE, I'M HUNGRY. LET'S GET OUT OF HERE! LET'S EAT!
creak
slam

prick
prick
FLASH
prick
throb, throb
creak
slam
prick

THAT'S IT. IT'S REALLY GETTING ON MY NERVES.
HEY, CAN I HAVE THAT BAND-AID? ...I THINK IT'S BEST TO PUT ONE ON AFTER ALL.
SURE.
rip
wrap

You have to lose it to know it. That's brutal.

With that said, there's simply no way to always be conscious of everything you're grateful for and could lose.

Is this why we all create some kind of distance?

pulls

rustle,
rustle

flushhh

click
WHAT'S THAT SMELL?
OH!
ME NEXT, ME NEXT! PLEASE DO MY NAILS TOO!
YEAH, SURE I CAN BUT

WHAT ABOUT THAT FINGER?
OH.
riiip
...COULD I GET ONE MORE BAND-AID?
TAKE AS MANY AS YOU WANT.
MODI

Beeep
I THINK IT'S DONE. YOU CAN TAKE IT OUT NOW.
ARE YOU SURE YOU ONLY WANT ONE NAIL DONE? I'M HAPPY TO DO THE REST.
NAH, I'M GOOD.
rustle
riiip
wrap
?
THIS IS PERFECT.
flop

How To Create A Full Braid Using Hair Ties

Our excuse for meeting today is the necklace.

How To Create A Full Braid Using Hair Ties

Near the top of your crown, gather hair from both sides and tie two strands together like doing a half-up, half-down look, one on top of the other.

Divide the top section in half and tie it underneath the second section by wrapping around it.

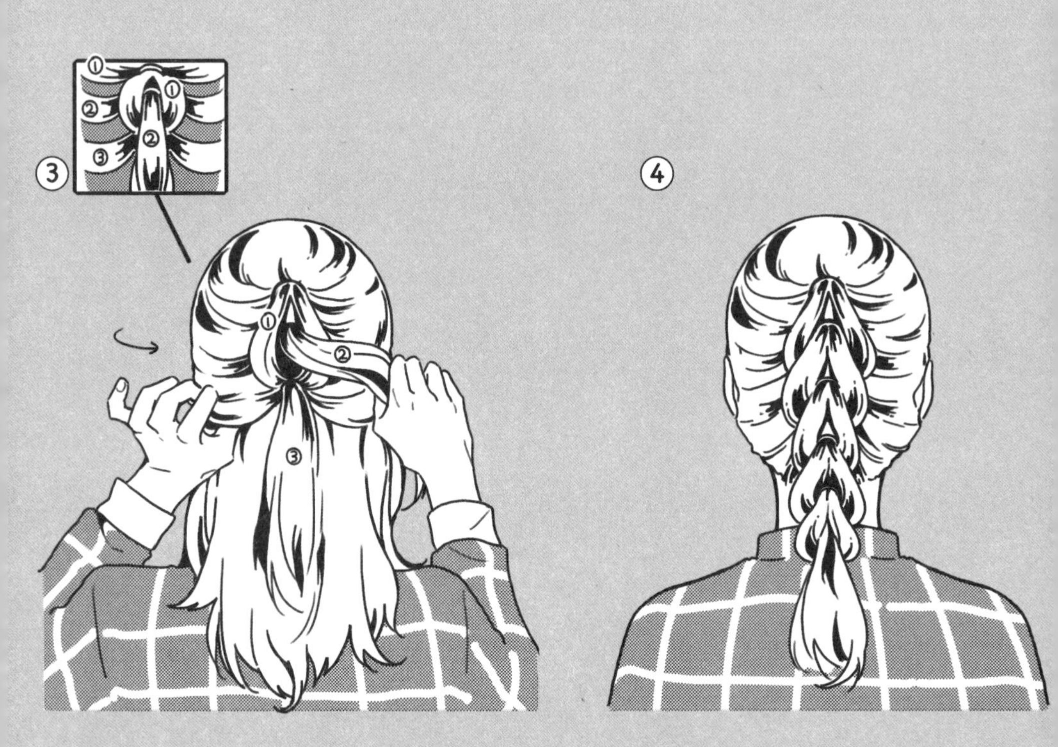

Underneath the second section, once again gather the hair from both sides like you're doing a half-up, half-down look, then combine the third section with the hair that wrapped around the second section from the first section. (Combine and tie sections 1 and 3 together.)

Repeat the steps until there's no hair remaining.

If there's any remaining hair, braid it or pull on the sections to make it look natural.

6

The more you pull on the sections to create a fuller feel, the prettier it looks. If there's a part that looks like it's lacking volume, it's good to pull out some wisps to create some curls.

WE'LL PROBABLY CHAT FOR A WHILE AT THE CAFÉ SO,
WE SHOULD PICK A PLACE THAT HAS COMFORTABLE SEATS.
tap, tap
Someplace that's not too small,
with plush cushioned chairs.
The taste of the coffee and the baked goods is a bit less important.
tap
gasp

HAHA, IT'S ME, IT'S ME.
HEY! HUH? YOUR HAIR!!
GUESS WHAT? I'VE RESIGNED FROM MY JOB.
WHAT? REALLY!?
DVD
P·T
공인중개사
Coffee
스시돈가스
Cafe

OH NO.
ALL THE SOFT CHAIRS SEEM TO BE TAKEN...
OH WELL...
NOTHING TO BE DONE. LET'S SIT HERE FOR NOW.
YEAH.
slip
OH, RIGHT. HERE.
SHUFFLE
BEFORE I FORGET. HERE'S WHAT YOU LEFT BEHIND LAST TIME.
AH, THANK YOU.

SO WHAT HAPPENED? YOU'RE NOT WORKING AT THE COMPANY ANYMORE?
rip
PULL
pop
AS MUCH AS I WISH THAT WERE THE CASE...
FOR A MONTH OR TWO, I NEED TO ONBOARD THE PERSON WHO'LL TAKE OVER MY JOB SO I'LL BE A LITTLE BUSY.
STILL, AFTER THAT'S ALL DONE I SHOULD HAVE SOME TIME TO MYSELF.
YOU'VE BEEN THROUGH SO MUCH... YOU MADE THE RIGHT CHOICE. REALLY.
...I WANTED TO STOP FEELING APOLOGETIC.
WHEN I LOOKED BACK ON THINGS, I REALIZED I WAS LIVING EVERY DAY FEELING SORRY.

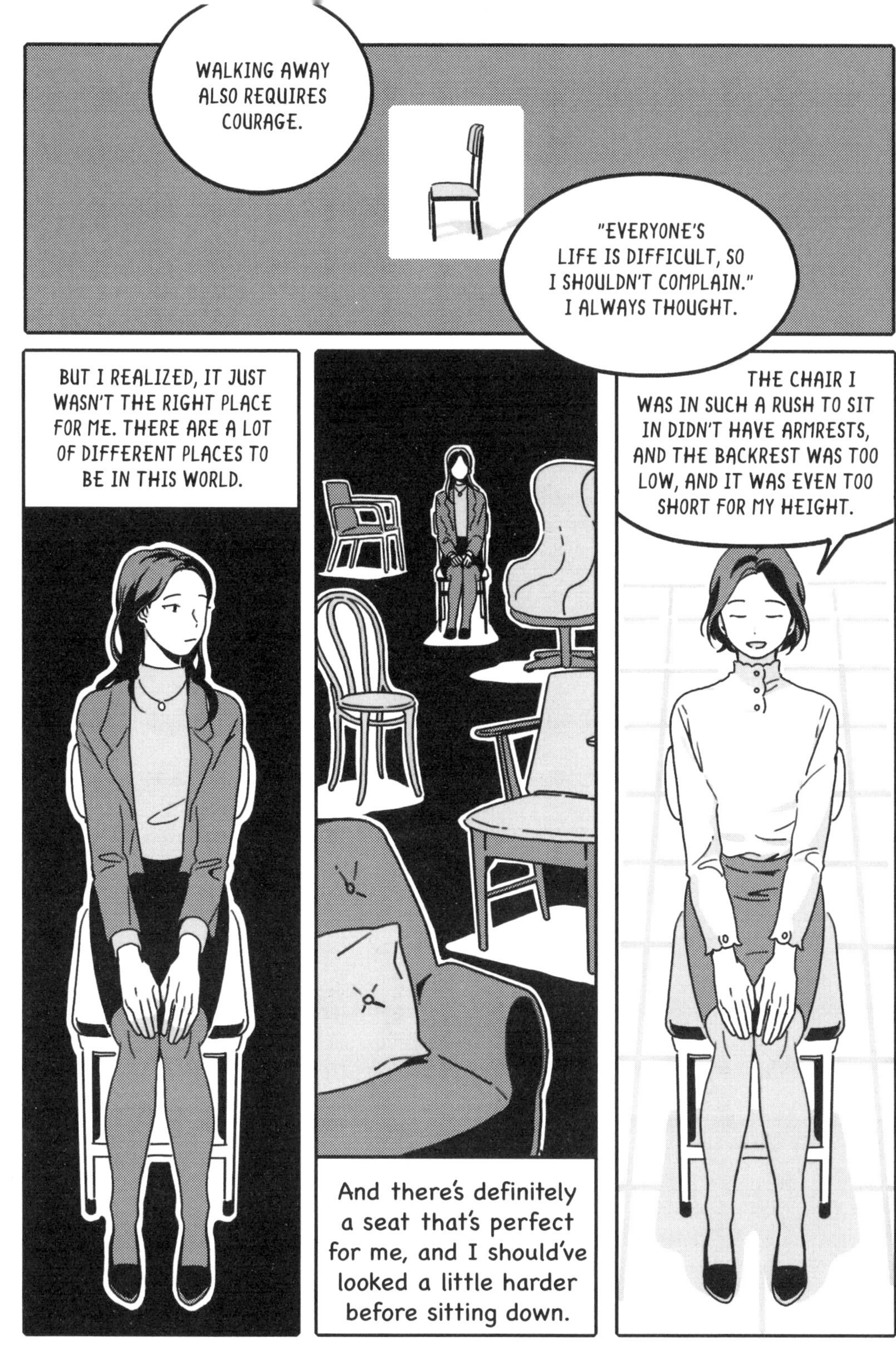
WALKING AWAY ALSO REQUIRES COURAGE.
"EVERYONE'S LIFE IS DIFFICULT, SO I SHOULDN'T COMPLAIN." I ALWAYS THOUGHT.
BUT I REALIZED, IT JUST WASN'T THE RIGHT PLACE FOR ME. THERE ARE A LOT OF DIFFERENT PLACES TO BE IN THIS WORLD.
And there's definitely a seat that's perfect for me, and I should've looked a little harder before sitting down.
THE CHAIR I WAS IN SUCH A RUSH TO SIT IN DIDN'T HAVE ARMRESTS, AND THE BACKREST WAS TOO LOW, AND IT WAS EVEN TOO SHORT FOR MY HEIGHT.

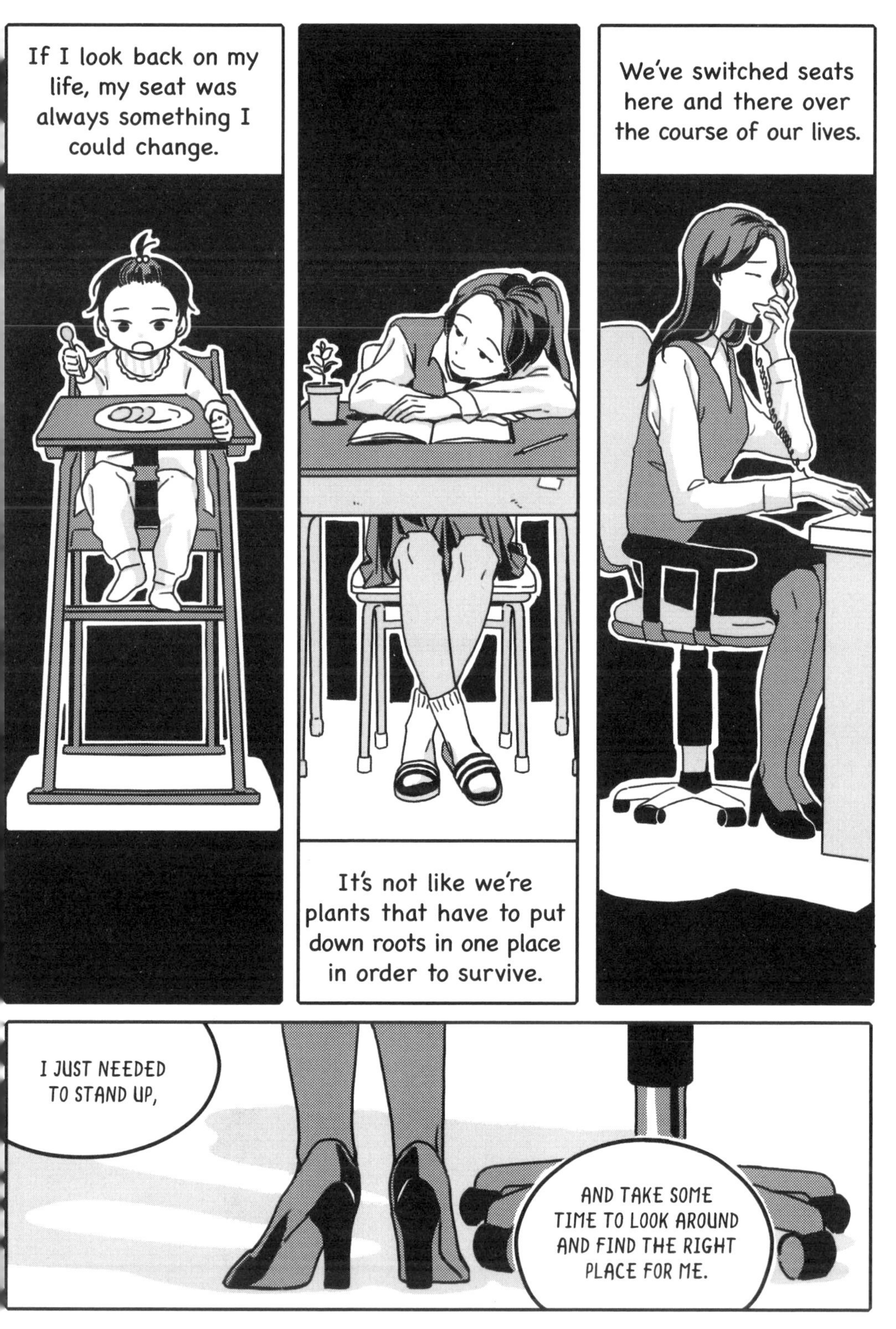
If I look back on my life, my seat was always something I could change.
It's not like we're plants that have to put down roots in one place in order to survive.
We've switched seats here and there over the course of our lives.
I JUST NEEDED TO STAND UP,
AND TAKE SOME TIME TO LOOK AROUND AND FIND THE RIGHT PLACE FOR ME.

...I SEE.
OH, WAIT A SECOND.
Hm?
TADA!
WHAT'S THIS?
CHEESECAKE. YOUR RESIGNATION GIFT.
ARE YOU SURE YOU DIDN'T JUST GET THEM BECAUSE YOU WANTED SOME?

From now on, you have to be careful not to be swayed by the "maybes".
cut
slide
Don't ever regret your decision.
...THIS IS MY GIFT TO ENCOURAGE YOU TO FIRMLY STAND YOUR GROUND.
yum
THANKS, I APPRECIATE IT.
IT'S DEFINITELY HARD TO CHEER FOR SOMEONE OR TO ENCOURAGE THEM IN THE RIGHT WAY.

SO WHAT ARE YOU GOING TO DO AFTER YOU RESIGN?
I CAN'T JUST STAND IN ONE SPOT AND WALK IN CIRCLES,
SO I'LL SLOWLY LOOK FOR ANOTHER SEAT, I GUESS.
I KNOW IT'LL BE HARD TO FIND THE RIGHT PLACE FOR ME RIGHT AWAY BUT,
RING
OH!

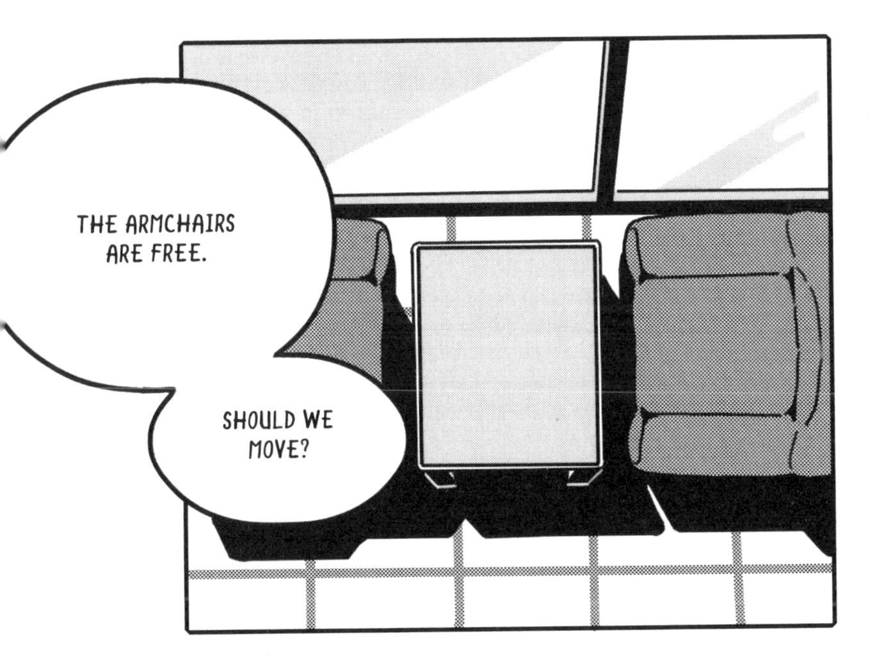
THE ARMCHAIRS ARE FREE.
SHOULD WE MOVE?

WOW. EAGLES' EYES.
SURE...
haha
I THINK YOU'LL FIND IT SOON. THE PLACE THAT'S JUST RIGHT FOR YOU.

How To Do A Crown Braid

Spring is coming.

Spring in Korea is a season where you can experience spring, summer, and winter all in one day.

Just when it gets warm enough for it to be nice out, it'll be summer all of the sudden.

A little while ago, while returning from grocery shopping I watched them trim the branches of the trees lining the streets.

crack
Trimming the branches is usually done before the new leaves emerge in the spring.
It's a little sad to see the thin branches being cut away after enduring the winter but

because the lower branches don't get much sunlight they lose their ability to photosynthesize, so they die easily
it's apparently better to trim them away with the dead branches.
AREN'T THEY CUTTING AWAY TOO MANY OF THEM?
crack
...Whatever, I guess just leaving things as they are isn't always for the best.

I SEE...
THAT'S WHY I'M DOING IT.
OH?
IT'S SIMILAR TO HAIR.
SINCE THE HAIR IS DAMAGED AND HAS SPLIT ENDS, IT SHOULD BE TRIMMED SO THAT IT CAN GROW BETTER.
flap
PARDON?
...SO WHAT YOU SAID EARLIER BOTHERED ME A BIT.
......
I REALLY DON'T UNDERSTAND WHY PEOPLE ASSUME WHEN A GIRL CUTS HER HAIR THAT SHE BROKE UP WITH SOMEONE, OR WAS DUMPED...

IS THIS OKAY FOR THE LENGTH?
NO, COULD YOU CUT A LITTLE BIT MORE?
OKAY, HOW ABOUT THIS LENGTH?
NO, A LITTLE MORE.
COULD YOU PLEASE CUT IT JUST LONG ENOUGH FOR ME TO TIE?

snip
DON'T YOU FIND IT A WASTE TO CUT YOUR HAIR?
snip
snip
plop
plop
IT'LL GROW AGAIN, SO NOT REALLY.

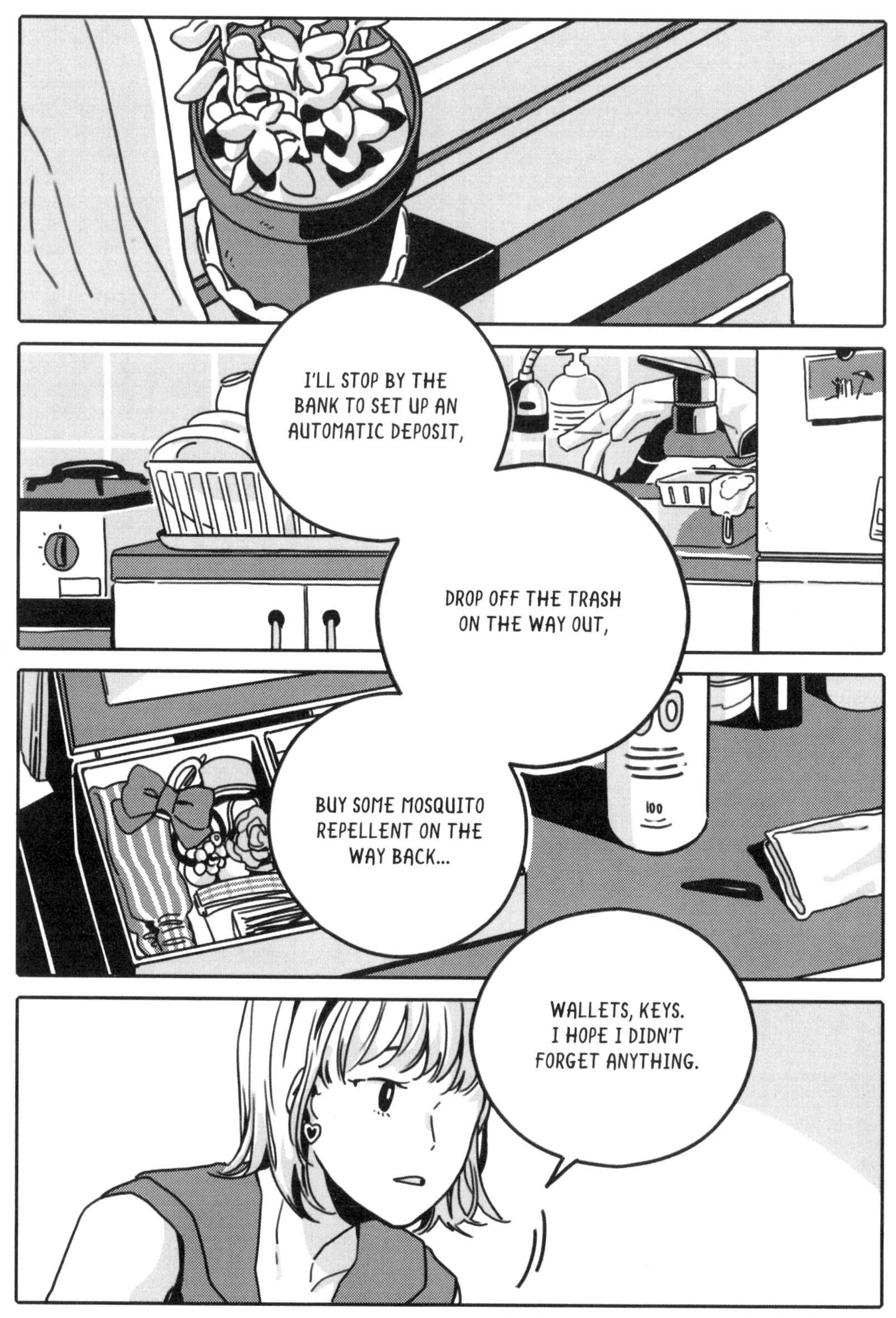
I'LL STOP BY THE BANK TO SET UP AN AUTOMATIC DEPOSIT,
DROP OFF THE TRASH ON THE WAY OUT,
BUY SOME MOSQUITO REPELLENT ON THE WAY BACK...
WALLETS, KEYS. I HOPE I DIDN'T FORGET ANYTHING.

IT FEELS A LITTLE WEIRD BECAUSE IT FEELS SO LIGHT ALL OF THE SUDDEN, BUT IT'LL PROBABLY GROW BACK AGAIN SOON.
I'LL TRY A LOT OF DIFFERENT THINGS AS I GROW IT OUT AGAIN.

How To Do A Crown Braid

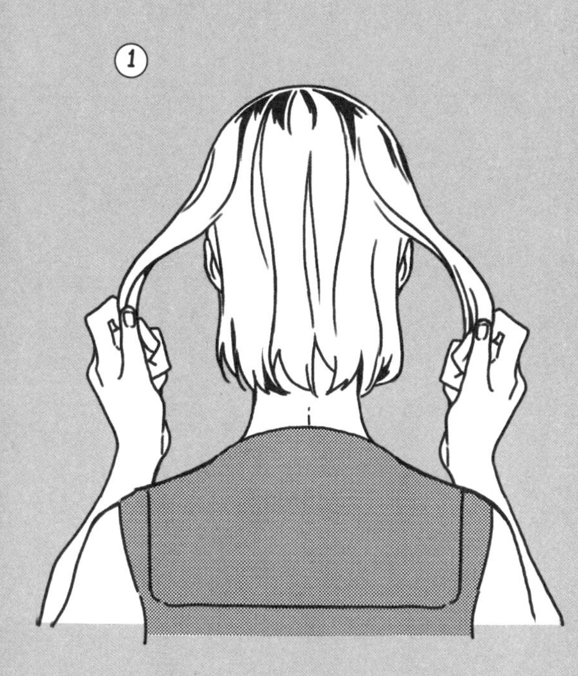

Take the hair from the sides near the crown of the head, leaving the hair in the back of the head, to create three sections.

One side at a time, braid the side pieces as if you're wrapping around the head and pull in pieces of hair as you do.

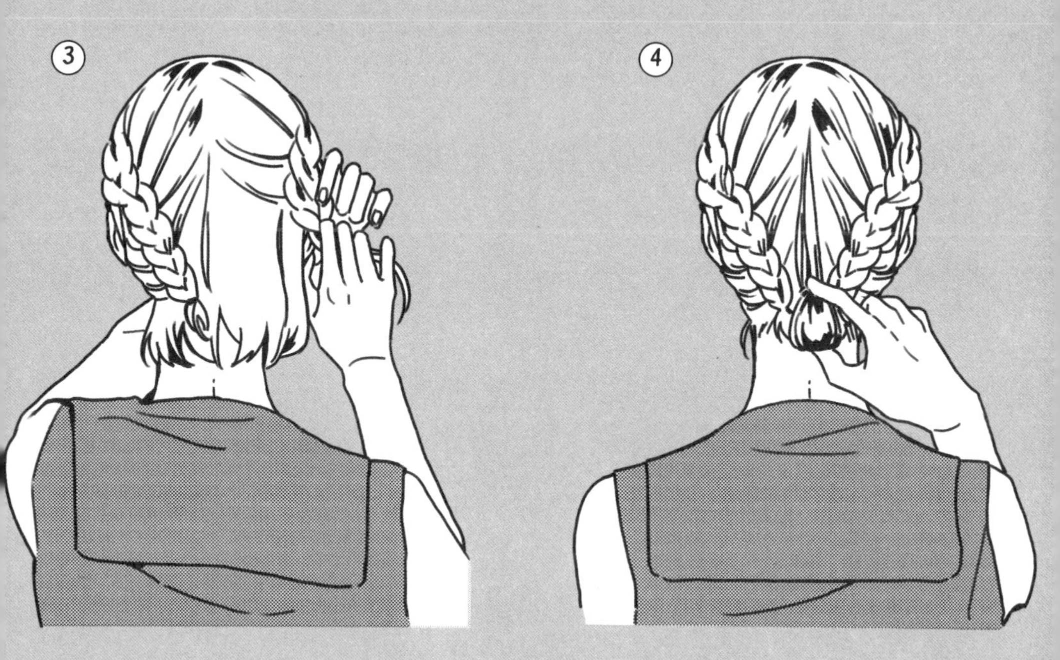

When you're finished braiding, tie with a hair tie. Then do the same on the other side, braid as if you're wrapping around the head.

Once you finish the braids, gather the remaining hair in the back to make a small ponytail.

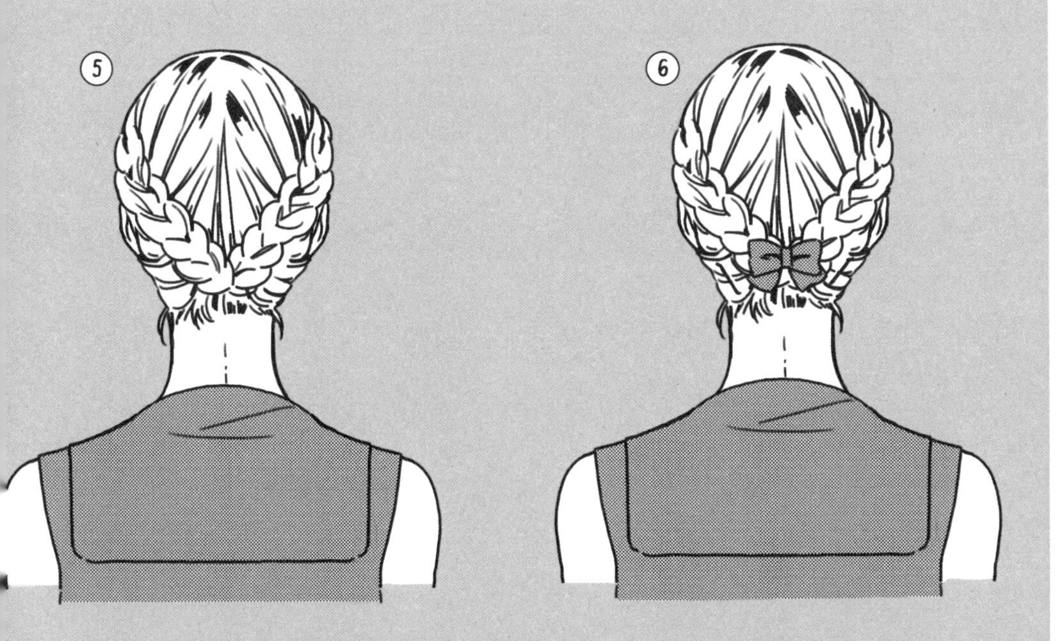

Tuck the small ponytail on the inside and fix the two braids over it using bobby pins.

You can finish neatly as is or add a small hair clip.

The seasons keep repeating, but the people keep changing.

엄마
Mom
????
Mom and dad took up hiking. I'm not sure how long it'll last.
One friend got lasik eye surgery. She said it's been fifteen years since she's walked around without glasses.
My other friend was promoted. She was always hard-working so I knew things would turn out for the best.
Then, there's the friend who's taking it easy while doing what she likes, unlike before. These days, she's studying to get certified in something that really interests her.
00:00

And finally there's me…
I cut my hair.
SHOULD WE HEAD OUT TO GET SOMETHING TO EAT? I FOUND A GOOD RESTAURANT.
SURE.
So what if it's a small, tiny change?
ring
Anyways, without our realizing it, many things are changing.
After all, if everything stays the same, life's no fun.
The End.

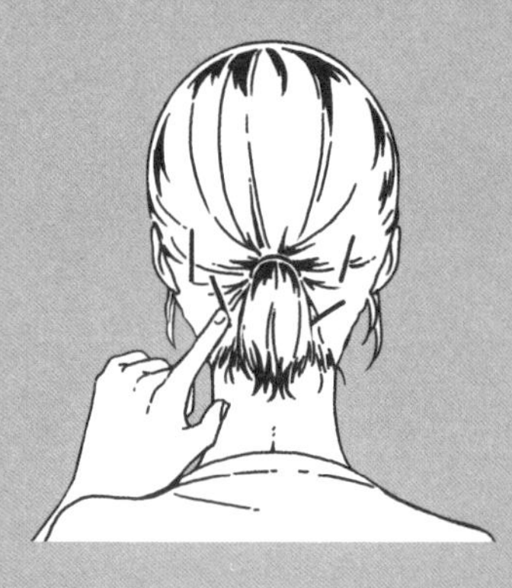

① How To Tie Short Hair

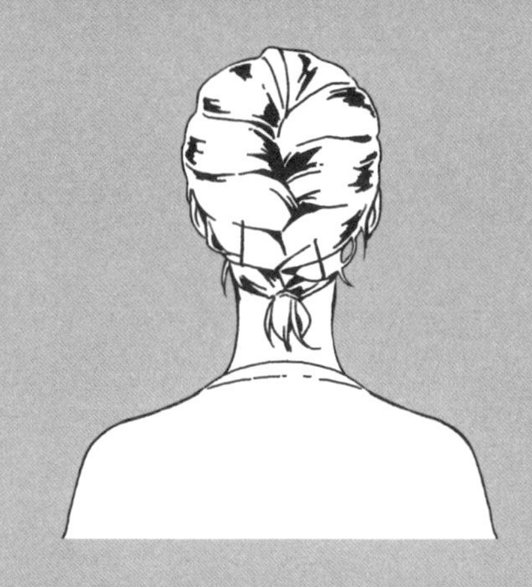

② How To French Braid Short Hair

③ How To Do A Half-Up Half-Down Hairstyle For Short Hair

④ How To Tie Pigtails With A Twist

⑤ How To Tie Hair Without A Hair Tie

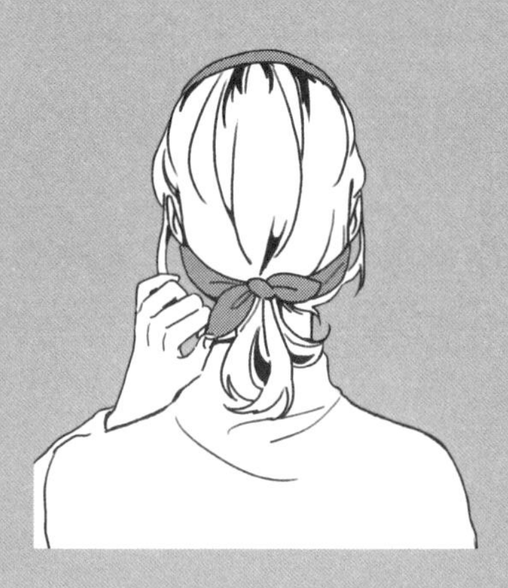

⑥ How To Tie Your Hair Using A Scarf

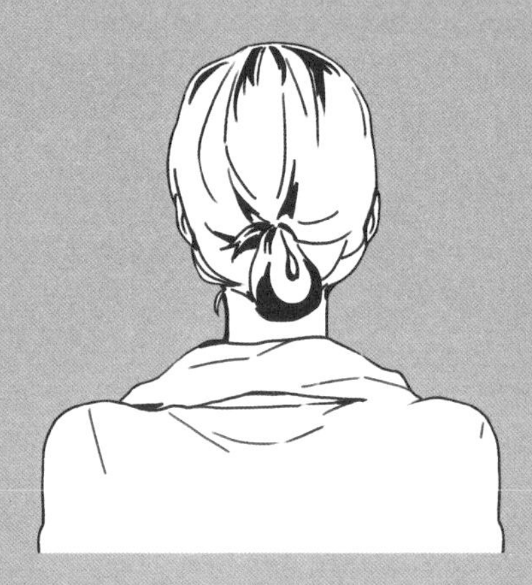

⑦ How To Tie Your Hair Mom's Way

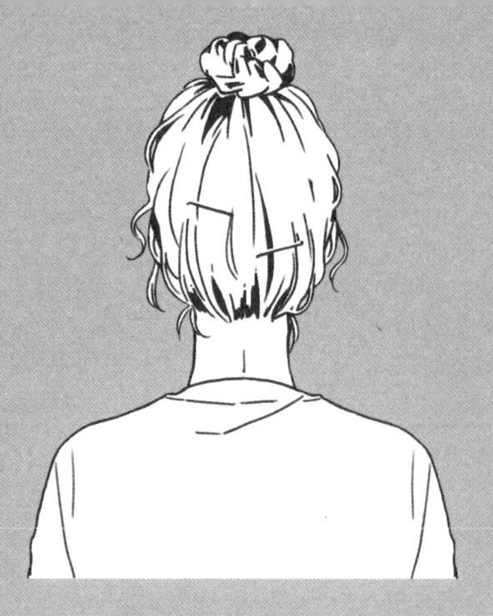

⑧ How To Tie Your Hair In A Comfortable Bun

⑨ How To Tie A Ponytail For Long Hair

⑩ How To Do A French Fishtail Braid

⑪ How To Create A Full Braid Using Hair Ties

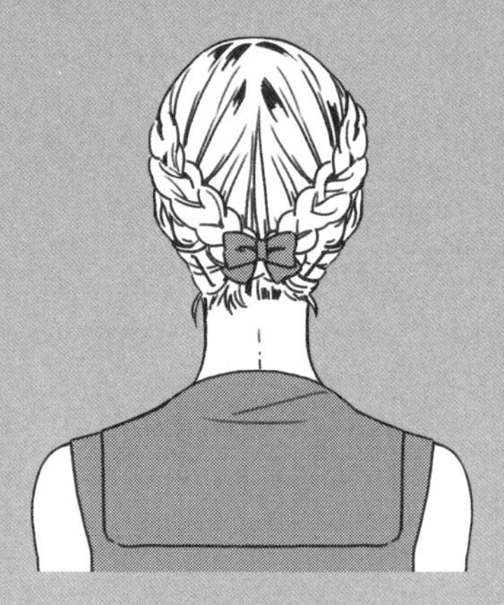

⑫ How To Do A Crown Braid

"Books to Span the East and West"

Tuttle Publishing was founded in 1832 in the small New England town of Rutland, Vermont [USA]. Our core values remain as strong today as they were then—to publish best-in-class books which bring people together one page at a time. In 1948, we established a publishing outpost in Japan—and Tuttle is now a leader in publishing English-language books about the arts, languages and cultures of Asia. The world has become a much smaller place today and Asia's economic and cultural influence has grown. Yet the need for meaningful dialogue and information about this diverse region has never been greater. Over the past seven decades, Tuttle has published thousands of books on subjects ranging from martial arts and paper crafts to language learning and literature—and our talented authors, illustrators, designers and photographers have won many prestigious awards. We welcome you to explore the wealth of information available on Asia at **www.tuttlepublishing.com**.

Published by Tuttle Publishing, an imprint of Periplus Editions (HK) Ltd.

www.tuttlepublishing.com

아주 약간의 변화

Originally published by YOUR-MIND

This English edition is published by arrangement with YOUR-MIND through BC Agency, Seoul
Translated from Korean by Seowan (Angela) Lee

ISBN: 978-0-8048-5708-6

Library of Congress Cataloging-in Publication Data is in process.

Distributed by
North America, Latin America & Europe
Tuttle Publishing
364 Innovation Drive
North Clarendon
VT 05759-9436, USA
Tel: 1 (802) 773 8930
Fax 1 (802) 773 6993
info@tuttlepublishing.com
www.tuttlepublishing.com

Asia Pacific
Berkeley Books Pte. Ltd.
3 Kallang Sector #04-01
Singapore 349278
Tel: (65) 67412178
Fax: (65) 67412179
inquiries@periplus.com.sg
www.tuttlepublishing.com

26 25 24 23 5 4 3 2 1

Printed in China 2309CM